LUNA STATION
QUARTERLY

Issue 047 | September 2021

Editor-in-Chief
Jennifer Lyn Parsons

Editors
Rocky Breen • Anna Catalano • Linda Codega
Wanda Evans • Angelica Fyfe • Cathrin Hagey
Sarah Pauling • Cait Ryan • Carly Racklin • Shana Ross
Gô Shoemake • Bridget Siniakov • Margaret Stewart • Izzy Varju

LUNA STATION PRESS
NEW JERSEY

Luna Station Quarterly publishes short fiction on March 1st, June 1st,
September 1st, and December 1st. For more information and submission
guidelines, please visit our website at lunastationquarterly.com

For Luna Station Press

Creative Director - Tara Quinn Lindsey
Editor-in-Chief & Founder - Jennifer Lyn Parsons

 LUNA STATION PRESS

www.lunastationpress.com

CONTENTS

Editorial

Jennifer Lyn Parsons

Jennifer Lyn Parsons is a writer, programmer, and maker. With influences ranging from Laura Ingalls Wilder to Jim Jarmusch, her tales feature a rare physicality with details that feel hand-carved. When not writing code or prose, she is also the editor-in-chief of the venerable Luna Station Quarterly. She finds joy in video games, comics books, discovering music new and old, and making things out of wool, paper, and wood.

It's amazing how the wheel of the year turns, the subtle shifts that happen right under our noses that are only visible when we pause after some time has passed and we find ourselves in a new season, with a new territory to navigate. Hopefully in that time we've also gathered some new wisdom to employ on the next step of our journeys.

When last we met, it was high Spring. Now it's high Summer here in the Northeast. There are boiling temperatures and humidity that makes you feel you're melting, but there are also tomatoes and peppers fresh from the garden. The foliage has deepened to that darker green that means it is no longer new, but middle aged and comfortable, though definitely not settled in its ways. Much like myself, if I'm honest.

Another change that has occurred since last we met is that I am once again writing. It's a relief and a joy. I wrote more about that shift on the LSQ blog if you're interested in following my journey. Suffice to say that I'm enjoying myself tremendously and I look forward to putting a few more nuggets of story out into the world soon. Hopefully, by the time you're reading this, a new issue of LSQ won't have been the only thing I've published this month.

Like many people, I've started reading James Clear's "Atomic Habits". He also has a weekly newsletter if you're like me and are into that kind of thing. Recently, in the newsletter he offered a piece of advice that I'm finding resonates with me:

"Pick a priority for this season of your life and do it to the best of your ability."

I've also become quite a fan of the RPG Wanderhome's unique months and seasons, which mirror my own, but from a new perspective. If I were there, I would be sitting in the month of Swarming, happy to be out of The Devildays, and very much looking forward to Gateling.

This all pulls together as I embrace my friends and our little circle's regular meetings to break bread. This year I am acknowledging the seasonal changes in a deeper way than ever before.

I am in the middle-age season of my life and I do not yet know what my priority is, though I think "deepening that which I am already doing" is probably a fair assessment of where I want to head.

LSQ is fully a part of that and I am so pleased to be able to share this collection of stories with you. Our authors have once again hit it out of the park. Once again we present to you a significantly large issue because we received yet another abundance of magnificent work that could be trimmed no further without losing something special, unique, and purely Luna Station Quarterly.

I hope you can find some space in your life to curl up with these tales and allow them to take you to new places. They will make you laugh, gasp, and shed a tear or two. I am still carrying them with me in my heart and I hope you find a place for them in yours. Enjoy.

L S Q | 047

No place like home

Rebecca Burton

Rebecca is a writer of SFF, a drinker of tea, and overly obsessed with Korean and Chinese dramas.

Maybe that was the noise Saffi had heard: the sound of Di's determination. It rang in her ears. Not the door slamming; Di hadn't slammed it, just let the automatic seals close behind her without a backward glance, but the sound echoed all the same.

Saffi's hands were curled into fists and the cut sapphires of Di's ring bit into her left palm. She straightened her stiff fingers and let the ring slip loose, onto the low coffee table which sat beside the sofa she had slumped down onto the moment Di had left. Her wife's parting words repeated themselves over and over, a descant to the pounding in her skull.

"When you join me in the city, I'll put it back on," Di had said, eyes bright and hard. "But, if you stay here..." She'd paused, refusing to meet Saffi's gaze, turned away to display her profile to perfection. Then her jaw had clenched, and she'd spat her last words to fall into the silence of Saffi's bewilderment. "Well, it would be best if we parted, I think."

Then, turning and picking up her handbag and one small holdall, she had walked out into the sunshine. The door had slid shut behind her, shutting out the light, and Saffi had stumbled backward until her calves hit the couch and she fell into it.

Time had slipped and now the afternoon was nearly over. And

it had only been 9am when Di had appeared with that damned holdall and a ticket back to the city in her hand.

Blindly, Saffi worked the ring off her own calloused finger and dropped it on the table beside Di's while her mind raced back to Core City eleven months ago and another ticket that had been grasped in that slim hand. A ticket to paradise, or so Di had said.

* * *

Saffi was slouching in the bio-form couch clutching a margarita and staring at the sky-cars whizzing past their apartment window when Di got home from work. On the 75th floor, high above the smog and with a view all the way to the ocean, it had cost more than they could really afford. But they had everything they could want—fresh food from the robotic farms that covered Felicity's southern continent; clothes, books and films, imported and Felicitean—even friends close by in the same tower.

She raised her glass in a toast to her wife, new wedding ring glinting in the light.

"Hey, hun. Fancy a drink before we go to Alastair's party tonight? I bought fresh limes."

Di waved away the suggestion, slipping off her heels and slumping into the other couch, a strip of plas-film clutched in one hand. "Saf, I—" she started, before pausing to stare out the window for a moment. "Do you mind if we don't go? There's something I wanted to talk to you about." She fiddled with her ring, a matching shape to Saffi's, but with blue stones gleaming rather than diamonds flashing.

"What's wrong?" Saffi leaned forward to put a hand on her wife's knee. "Of course, we don't have to go if you don't want to. Did something happen at work?"

Di shrugged. "Sorta. Nothing big, but it's just one thing after another, you know?"

Saffi nodded. Di hadn't been happy for a while—dreading going into the office and coming home a washed-out pencil drawing of her usual self. She'd buried the knowledge of it under the excitement of planning their wedding, but she couldn't deny that her wife was depressed any longer.

"I can't keep doing this. I just want to run away. Please don't make me go back." Tears streamed down Di's cheek and Saffi jumped up to pull her into a hug.

"You don't have to do anything you don't want, love. It's all right. We'll fix it. We'll find you a new job somewhere. A better one."

"No." Di pulled away from her. "I'm leaving. I want you to come with me. But either way, I have to get out of here. I can't take it anymore." She covered her face in her hands, the plas-film sheet still held tightly in one fist.

Saffi frowned as she looked around their apartment, the one they had spent so much time and money finding. They'd only just got the life they'd been dreaming of since college. Why would Di want to leave now?

"But where do you want to go, love?"

Di thrust the hand holding the plas-film at her.

Taking the crumpled sheet, Saffi unfolded it and stared at the flyer.

"No. You can't be serious?" She laughed. It must have been some kind of joke.

But Di dropped her hands and glared at her. "I am deadly fucking serious."

"You want to go North? You want to live in the Shear Zone? What the hell, Di?"

North: Felicity's second, smaller continent, un-terraformed and given over to reserves to preserve the planet's native wildlife—and tourist lodges and hotels so people could visit and gawk. And one small strip of land between the sea and the endless forests where die-hard luddites and anti-social, bull-headed settlors scraped a living from the soil. The Shear Zone, star of a hundred novels and films where gender stereotypes ruled and life was cheap.

Saffi wasn't sure whether to laugh or cry.

"I'm going, Saf. With or without you." Di's jaw was set. When she looked like that, there was no arguing with her. Saffi had learnt that long ago.

"But, how? Neither of us know how to farm. And where are we going to buy tractors and chickens and all that shit?"

A small smile curled up one corner of Di's mouth. "It's all taken care of. The Settler Corporation provides everything we need: transport, a plot of land and a house, seeds, animal stock. Tutorials. And if we don't like it, we can come home." She reached out to hold Saffi's hand. "We have a year in our contract to give it all up and come back south, or decide to stay."

"And we get our apartment back if we quit?"

Di grimaced. "Not exactly. We transfer the apartment to them as payment for the package. But if we come back, they'll find us somewhere else to live. And it wouldn't be hard to get a job. Not with your qualifications."

"I'm not sure, Di. I'm a city girl. I like it here. I've never lived anywhere else! Aren't there other options we can try first? You could retrain. Start over with a different company."

Di leaned back to stare out the window again, refusing to meet Saffi's eyes. "I already signed the papers," she murmured.

"What?"

Di flushed. "I'm sorry! I got so excited about it and I didn't think. But it's for the best. This is a new start for us. A new life to go with our new start." Di pulled Saffi into her lap and twined their left hands together so their matching rings met.

Saffi stared at their joined hands and knew, as she had known ten years ago when they'd first met, that she couldn't say no to this woman.

"All right. We'll give it a try. If it will make you happy."

"You won't regret it. I promise." Di's voice brightened with excitement as she listed all the things they would need to do and pack before they left while Saffi stared out of the window and thought of all the things she was going to miss.

* * *

The chime of the doorbell brought Saffi back to the present, and she scrubbed the tears from her cheek before answering.

Ivy's face filled the narrow gap in the doorframe that Saffi allowed to open. "Hey, neighbour!" she said, then her face stilled as she got a good look at Saffi. "Oh dear, darling. What happened? The new clutch of crocahens didn't all die, did they?" As she spoke, she bustled through the doorway and laid a handmade basket down on the table next to the rings before turning to face Saffi again, hands on hips.

"No, no, nothing like that." Saffi stumbled over the words, her tongue thick from crying. "The chicks are all doing fine."

"Well, then, what's got you looking like a wet weekend in harvest-time?" Ivy frowned. "Bobby said he saw Di in town heading for the shuttle-port. Has she gone back to visit her folks? I daresay you'll miss her while she's gone."

A peal of harsh laughter spilled from Saffi's throat. "She's not coming back."

"Well, no wonder then." Ivy narrowed her eyes as she inspected Saffi and the state of the living room. "And you've been sitting there ever since she left, not moving. Am I right? I thought the yard looked a mess when I parked up."

Saffi's head drooped on her neck, too heavy to hold up. "Something like that."

Ivy sat down next to her on the worn sofa and reached out to pat her hand. "Why don't you come over to ours for dinner tonight? You look like you could use a good meal and a distraction. My eldest is home from the city and we're having a big meal to celebrate. That's why I stopped by, to invite you."

The unsaid "both" hung in the air between them.

"Unless you're leaving too?" she added softly.

Saffi dragged a hand across her eyes. "I don't know. I have no idea what I'm going to do now."

"Don't fret about it, dearie. Come to dinner. It won't look so bad on a full belly and a good night's sleep. There's no hurry to decide, after all."

"No, I guess not." Saffi sniffed and nodded. "All right. I'll come over. Thank you, Ivy."

"You're welcome, darling. Any time. And let us know if you're struggling here on your own. I'll send my boys over to help with the chores whenever you need."

Saffi managed a smile. "As if you don't need them working on your own land."

Ivy started to reply, but Saffi raised a hand to stop her. "I appreciate the offer. I really do. I'll let you know if I need the help." *If I stay,* she thought. *If I follow Di back to the city again, it doesn't much matter if the chores get done or all the crops die.*

"I'd better get back and start cooking," Ivy said, rising to her feet and pulling Saffi into a hug. "There's a cake in that basket for you and a bottle of my best damson wine. Have a bite now, and bring the basket back with you tonight." Smiling and wagging a finger at Saffi, she disappeared through the door into the setting sun outside.

Saffi sank back into the sofa with a sigh. She wasn't sure she was up to an evening with the rowdy Andersen family. But if she didn't go, Ivy was as like as not to send one of her sons to fetch her. Just like she'd done their first day in the Shear.

* * *

It wasn't the most prepossessing sight.

The shuttle had dropped them off in town—if you could call ten clapboard buildings a town—and they'd picked up their buggy and supplies at the trading post. Two hours of bumping across non-existent roads later and here they were.

"Welcome home, Saf!" Di squealed as she leapt out of the buggy. "Our own twenty acres of heaven."

More like twenty acres of dirt and rotten fences, Saffi thought, glancing around the tumbledown farm yard. She hoped the house was in a better state, or at least slightly cleaner.

Di grabbed her hand and tugged her forward. "Let's check out the barn. Our droids should be around here somewhere."

Saffi allowed herself to be pulled into the nearest building. Blinking as her eyes adjusted, she made out a huge machine taking up a full third of the hanger. It was silent and still, but the sheer size of it was menacing.

"That's our harvester," Di said, staring up at it in

awe. She flipped though the manual she held in her free hand. "It's a HAWS: Heavy Agricultural Work System," she read. "Let's call it Horse for short."

"Sure, if you want." Saffi tried to sound interested, but was pretty sure she'd failed. She thought of their comfortable, clean apartment in the City and grimaced. "I'm going to go check out the house. See you inside in a bit?"

"Uh-huh," Di replied, absorbed in the interface for the Horse. "See you soon, love."

Saffi shook her head as she walked away. It was good to see Di so happy for a change, but she wasn't overly optimistic that this would work out in the long run. As least they could still go back home if they changed their minds.

The inside of the house was even worse than she expected. Pushing the door open, she coughed as a cloud of dust engulfed her. The floor, the walls, even the windows were coated in it. In a way, it was lucky there was very little furniture that she could see, otherwise that would have been covered in dust too.

A saggy couch sat in the middle of the room with a small table next to it. Through an arch on the other side of the room, Saffi could see cupboards, a sink, and a cooking unit coated in more dust and grime, and there was a single door to her left that, presumably, led to the bedroom and bathroom.

Wrinkling her nose, Saffi walked through to the small kitchen, looking for a broom or a hi-vac or something she could use to start cleaning up. Back home, the house droids had taken care of keeping their apartment clean and tidy, but she had to assume there weren't any here—the dust told her that.

The kitchen proving empty of anything useful, Saffi turned to the door in the inside wall. She expected a pantry or a broom closet, but she found a set of stairs leading down into darkness, walls festooned in crawler webs.

Pulling her sleeve up over her hand, she reached out and flicked the light switch. Dim bulbs glowed at the bottom of the stairs, dull behind their coating of web. Soft skitterings marked the exodus of crawlers as they scrambled for the shadow.

"Fuck this shit," Saffi muttered, but she stepped forward into the gloom. There had to be some kind of cleaning equipment somewhere in this dump.

The bottom of the stairs opened out into a basement with a low ceiling. It seemed the same size as the house above, but it was hard to tell with all the boxes and junk piled up every which way. Saffi started poking around, looking for anything useful.

Pulling down one of the boxes, she spotted a figure behind it. With a shriek, she scrambled backward, falling on her butt on the filthy floor.

She cringed, looking up at the figure from behind her hands, but it didn't move.

Saffi clambered to her feet, heart beating fast, and tried to brush off some of the crud that clung to her clothes.

She stepped forward to better see the figure in the dim light and realised that it was a droid.

Reaching up, she felt for the power switch on the back of the unit's neck and flipped it on before hurrying back across the basement to the stairs.

There was a soft whirr as the droid booted up, then the LEDs on its face started to glow.

"Augmented Farm Unit online." Its voice buzzed in the close confines of the basement. "Powering up."

Its head moved back and forth, scanning the room. "Greetings, Em," it said to Saffi. "I am Unit 5489Za-9. Might I enquire as to the whereabouts of Em Robbins?"

"Who?" Saffi asked.

"My owner and the owner of this farmstead," it replied.

"Oh. I think he's dead? Or he might have just left and gone back to the City. They didn't really tell us much."

"Are you the new owner of this farmstead and this unit."

"Er, yes. I guess. Di and I just arrived. The company said this plot was ours."

"Welcome, Em. I am sorry I was not available to greet you or to maintain the house for your arrival. Em Robbins did not appreciate my presence and requested that I turn myself off." The droid seemed almost rueful and Saffi couldn't repress a smile.

"You're very formal, aren't you?" she said.

The droid looked almost affronted. "My database

contains social customs from all sections of society, Em. I am programmed to adapt to my owner's habits and expectations."

Saffi laughed. "I suppose that's good, then. I think we're gonna need your help. It's a bit of a state up there."

"It is my pleasure to serve." The droid clanked forward, extricating itself from the piled boxes. "In order to complete the ownership transfer, please may I scan your ID."

"Sure." Saffi held out her wrist and the droid extended a small probe that passed over her skin.

"Thank you, Em Sapphire. Ownership change processing." The LEDs flashed red, then green. "Ownership transferred. How might I serve you today?"

"If you could help us get the house vaguely habitable, that would be a great start. We'll need somewhere to sleep tonight!"

"Of course, Em. Please lead the way upstairs."

Saffi emerged into daylight to find Di standing in the middle of the kitchen, a huge smile on her face.

"Isn't this amazing, Saf? All this space!" She spun on the spot, arms raised, but stopped as the droid emerged into the light. "Another droid. This must be our augmented unit."

"Yeah, I found it switched off in the basement. It's full of crawlers down there." Saffi shuddered.

"I shall ensure that they are removed, Em Sapphire,"

the droid said. "But first, allow me to clean the living quarters for you and Em Diamond."

Di beamed. "It's the best droid ever. So polite! We'll call you Augie."

"Yes, Em."

Saffi rubbed her forehead. Was she the only one here who saw what a state everything was in?

While Augie started cleaning up, Di dragged Saffi back outside. "There's a lot to do, I know," she said, rubbing Saffi's arm with one hand. "But it's going to be amazing. I can see it now. Our own cows in the fields and wheat swaying in the breeze. Chickens in the farmyard and laundry drying on the line. It'll be just like a storybook."

"Yeah, Di. Course." Saffi kicked at the dirt with the toe of one of her brand-new boots. They were already pinching her feet. Then a flash of light caught her eye and her head whipped up. "What's that?"

Di peered up the road. "It looks like a buggy. But who would be coming to visit us?"

"Oh, god," Saffi groaned.

"What?"

"That awful woman from the trading post. The one who was so snooty about the chickens we picked up. She said she'd send her son to bring us over for dinner. Interfering old busybody."

Di glanced from their still-loaded buggy into the

kitchen where Augie was splashing around water and soap. "Well, a free meal wouldn't go amiss. It's not like we've unpacked yet, and I don't want to eat in there. Do you?"

Saffi wrinkled her nose. "No."

"Come on. She seemed nice to me. It'll be fun." Di swung her arms, pulling Saffi's with her. "Gotta meet the neighbours some time."

Saffi pouted. "Fine. But I still think she's a busybody."

Di grinned and swept in to place a kiss on her cheek. "Thank you, love. I do appreciate you coming, you know."

"I know." Saffi smiled and swatted her wife's arm. "Now go be social. I'll catch up in a moment."

She leaned back against the wall of the house as Di raced off to greet the man in the buggy. So much for the start of their great adventure, she thought. But at least Di was happy.

* * *

The clomp-clank of Augie's footsteps on the wooden floor gave Saffi just enough warning to rub her eyes dry before the droid appeared in the kitchen doorway.

"Excuse me, Em Sapphire," they said, polite as ever. "But it is getting late and I could use your assistance in rounding up the crocahens. You know how they dislike being shut in for the night."

"Yes," Saffi said. Or tried to say but it came out as a croak, more like the sound of one of the pesky crocahens than human speech.

She cleared her throat and tried again. "I'll be right with you, Augie. Sorry. I lost track of time today."

"Not a problem, Em. Should I wait for you by the coop?"

"No, I'm coming. Just a moment." She scrubbed her face, hoping the droid hadn't noticed that she'd been crying. Did droids understand what crying was? And, more importantly, where the hell were her boots?

"To your left, Em." Augie pointed to where her rogue footwear was leaning against the side of the sofa. Of course, she'd kicked them off after Ivy left and the shock had worn off, leaving her in pieces.

Saffi grabbed the boots and shoved her feet in, not bothering about the laces. "Let's go then," she said.

"After you, Em," Augie replied, moving out of the doorway to give her space to precede them through the kitchen to the back door.

The sun hung low in the western sky as Saffi emerged blinking into what was left of the daylight. It felt like only minutes had passed since Di had left, but the day was nearly over. She'd planned to do so many things today: re-fencing the home 'lope pasture and planning next year's seed-crop. And all she'd actually done was cry and refuse to decide what she wanted to do.

Shaking off her thoughts, Saffi headed across the kitchen garden toward the farm's main yard. Barns lined three sides of the yard: the 'lope byre, the granary, and the machine store. The fourth side was open to the west, giving her a golden view across the pastures and the ploughed fields. It would have been breathtaking if there had been any air left in her lungs, but Di had already stolen it all with the suddenness of her departure. How could she have been so blind to her wife's unhappiness?

A voice called from the machine store. Horse was plugged in, recharging from the solar panels after a full day's work—at least someone was working—and they hailed her as she passed the door.

"Hi, Horse," Saffi replied, forcing a smile for the friendly droid. "Everything okay?" Augie followed her into the barn.

"Right as rain," Horse said. "All the wheat is in and I was gonna start on the corn tomorrow. Whaddya think?"

"Sure. Sounds like a great idea." Saffi paused, mulling over her next words. How to tell Horse that they should do what they thought best? They and Augie might have to run the farm by themselves for a while if she followed Di. It wouldn't do to let things go to complete wrack and ruin again until a new tenant arrived. It would take far more work to put things back into order than just to keep the farm ticking along. Crops and beasts waited on no woman.

But before she could line up the right way of saying things, Horse interrupted her.

"We heard, Augie and I...we heard Em Diamond went back to the city. Are you going too?"

Saffi laid a hand against Horse's side and leaned into their comforting weight. "I don't know. I haven't decided yet."

"I hope you don't. We'd miss you."

"I'd miss you too," she said, and realised that it was true. She would miss Augie and Horse, and Ivy and all of the Andersens, far more than she ever missed any of her city friends. But then there was Di to think of.

"Come, Em Sapphire," Augie interrupted her thoughts. "The light is fading."

"Oh, the crocahens. Yes." She pushed herself upright again and moved to the door. "But, call me Saffi. Please? Both of you." She glanced back at both droids, watching the lights on their fascia flashing in sequence.

"Affirmative, Em Saffie," Augie replied.

Saffi let out a pained laugh. "Not Em, just Saffi. We're family, right? Family doesn't need honorifics."

"All right, Saffi." Maybe she imagined it, but Augie's voice sounded warmer as they said her name freely for the first time. Maybe it was all in her head, but at least they *seemed* pleased.

"Will do, Saffi," Horse boomed from their corner of the barn. "Family... I like that."

The corner of Saffi's lips lifted at their enthusiasm and she thought how she'd have to tell Di about the droids' pleasure and persuade her to give up her Em too. Then she remembered and the nascent smile fell.

She spun and headed for the door again, not wanting Augie to see the tears in her eyes. "We'd better round up these damn crocahens then," she said brightly as Augie followed her back out into the daylight.

The cockerel, Seamus, was perched on top of the coop, scaly tail twitching, and refused to come down until they had rounded up all of his females and ushered them inside. As usual, Saffi suffered a few nips from the broody hens who didn't want to be parted from the eggs they had laid in bushes and, in one case, up on the axle of the buggy, but at last she shoved the final ungrateful hen into the house.

Seamus crowed to the setting sun and then fluttered down to land on her shoulder, rubbing his beak against her ear.

"I love you too, silly," she murmured to him, then plucked him off his perch and pushed him toward the coop door. "Off you go. You don't want to be eaten by a wolger, do you?"

He clucked crossly at her a couple of times and then minced into the darkness of the coop. Augie shut the door behind him.

"Intelligent bird," they said.

"Yes. Much brighter than those Earth chickens the company saddled us with. They barely lasted a week." How naïve they'd been when they first arrived. Thank goodness Ivy set them straight or they would have been back in the city within a month.

* * *

Saffi looked at the dead chicken cradled in Di's hands.

"That's the third one in two days," Di said, sighing. "What are we doing wrong?"

"The wheat's not growing either, Augie says," Saffi replied. "That woman was right. The company has given us crap."

Di frowned. "No, they wouldn't. They gave us every-thing we needed!" She paused. "But maybe it was only what they thought we needed," she added in a softer voice, turning away to lay the chicken down next to its dead hatch-mates.

Saffi laid a hand on her wife's shoulder. "Don't cry, love."

"It's just not what I thought it would be like, you know,"

Di said, wiping away a tear. She offered Saffi a tremulous smile. "I wanted an adventure. I guess I got more of one than I bargained for."

"Go back in the house," Saffi said. "I'll deal with these... and then go and get some advice from Ivy. There must be something missing from the manuals." She pushed Di toward the house. "Rest. I'll take care of everything."

Di nodded and disappeared inside.

Saffi let out all of her breath in a rush. "Shit." She turned to Augie, who was waiting patiently beside her. "Do you think you could dispose of these please?" she asked the droid.

"Yes, Em. I will add them to the composter. Their lives will not be wasted." Augie bent and gathered up the limp bodies in their cold metal hands.

"I'm going to the Andersens," Saffi said. "Keep an eye on Di for me?"

"Of course, Em."

The journey to the Andersens farmstead took about thirty minutes in the buggy, bumping over the dusty roads. It gave Saffi too much time to think.

Di had been so happy when they arrived, but it had drained out of her gradually as more and more went wrong on their small farm. It was a different kind of sadness to how she'd been in the City: smaller, less angry, less hopeful. It hurt Saffi to watch her diminish like that.

But, at the same time, despite their failures, despite the dead chickens and the wheat that wouldn't sprout, there was something deeply satisfying to her here. Rising with the sun and digging her hands into the soil. And at least her veggie patch was doing well—even if nothing else was.

At last, the Andersens' trim farmhouse appeared from behind a small copse of tringa trees. Ivy would know what to do. Despite only having met the woman a few times, she was so competent and calm that Saffi knew she could be relied on.

With a brisk knock, Saffi stuck her head around the open kitchen door. "Helloo. Anyone home?"

"Sapphire, dear. An expected pleasure." Ivy beamed at her, dusting flour off her hands onto her apron. "Come in. There's a batch of biscuits in the oven. You must take some back for your lovely wife, too."

Saffi let herself be shepherded to a table and took the mug of coffee gratefully. They couldn't afford real coffee yet. Not with the farm running so poorly. Damn, she had missed it.

Ivy sat opposite, a slight frown on her face as she inspected Saffi. "Out with it, young woman. What's brought you all this way to see me?"

"It's all gone wrong, Ivy. The last chicken died this morning, none of our crops will grow, and Di..." Saffi swallowed. "I think I'm losing her. She's just fading. Right in front of my eyes."

"Oh, honey." Ivy moved around the table next to her

and wrapped an arm around her shoulders. "I know it's hard. It's always hard starting out. But you'll get through it. And we'll help."

"But why? What did we do wrong?"

"Nothing, dear. It's that rubbish the company foisted on you. Why would they ever think that Earth birds and crops would survive out here. We're not even terraformed!" Normally placid, Ivy's eyes flashed with anger.

But she turned calm again before Saffi could react. "Never mind that. I'll send you home with two of my crocahen pullets and a batch of eggs. You have an incubator, don't you?"

Saffi nodded.

"Good. They'll give you eggs, and meat too, eventually. And last much better than those stupid chickens. Then, you go into town, see Mac at the trade post. Tell him I sent you and that if he doesn't give you the good seedcrop, I'll tell Martha what he did last solstice festival."

Ivy stood, pulling a basket from under the sink and filling it with eggs and a parcel of fresh biscuits.

"Once you've got settled with that, you come back and I'll make my Isaac sell you a pair of 'lopes, with calves at foot. At cost. Better get your fencing fixed first, though. Old Man Robbins left it in a fine state and you don't want them to go feral on you." She passed the overflowing basket to Saffi with a smile. "Don't forget what I said about Mac, now. He can be a miserly old bugger."

"I…" Saffi paused to rub her eyes with her knuckles. "I don't know how to thank you, Ivy. This is too much."

"Nonsense, dear." Ivy pushed her out the door and toward the waiting buggy. "It's tough when you're starting out. We've all been there. You'll get your chance to help someone else out one day. Now, get going. You've got work to do."

"Yes, Ivy," Saffi said as she hauled herself back into the buggy, basket of food beside her and a crate of pullets at her feet that Ivy's droid had placed there.

She backed the buggy out of the yard and grinned as Ivy waved her off. This might not be quite how they planned it, but perhaps they could make their farm work after all. With a little help from their neighbours.

* * *

Augie tapped her on the shoulder. "Are you all right, Saffi?"

"Sorry. Lost in thought for a minute." She shook herself. This wasn't like her, to keep drifting off into the past, but she couldn't seem to stay grounded today.

"Shall I make you some dinner? Food might help." The droid sounded worried.

"No. Thank you, but I said I'd go to Ivy's tonight."

"An excellent idea. Should I ask Horse to take you over?"

"Don't bother Horse. They have another busy day tomorrow. I'll take the buggy." Saffi smiled at Augie and their mother-hen antics as she swung up into the buggy and set off. It was nice to know someone cared, even if it was only programming and wires. It felt like a long time since someone had worried about her.

The familiar landscape raced past as Saffi let her mind drift, barely seeing the road ahead, until the Andersen's farm-gate loomed in front of her and, with a jolt, she realised she had already arrived.

Ivy came bustling out of the kitchen. "There you are! We were starting to worry. Come inside. Dinner's nearly ready."

In a whirlwind of motion, Saffi's coat was taken away and she was seated at one end of the long dining table, a cold glass of homemade lemonade clutched in one hand. Ivy's eldest, Mason, sat at the head of the table to her left. The place of honour for the returning hero—if a ten-day journey to the City and back could be called heroic.

Mason grinned at her, raising his glass to clink against hers. "Saf, good to see you! Mum forgot to mention you were coming. No Di tonight?"

Saffi heard an indrawn breath from Ivy, who had just entered the room with a crock of stew grasped in her hands. She glanced over to see Ivy frantically grimacing at her eldest, trying to get him to stop talking, but Mason was oblivious.

"Old Mac mentioned he'd seen her getting on a shuttle when I passed through town," he continued. "Couldn't hack it any-more, I suppose? She never seemed like the farming type. Not like you."

Ivy had put down the stew and was wringing her hands, looking anxiously at Saffi.

I could lie, Saffi thought, *tell him Di's just gone for a visit. That she'll be back soon. Smooth everything over—for a bit, anyway.*

She shook her head and smiled at Mason. "Yes, she went back. I guess things didn't turn out quite how she hoped here. She was so excited to come, but farming is hard work."

"You can say that again," Isaac, Ivy's husband, murmured.

"But you'll be staying," Mason said. It wasn't a question. "You belong here, like us. The soil is in your bones."

"I don't know..." Saffi stared into the bowl of stew Ivy had slipped in front of her. "I—" She stopped herself. Was Mason right? She'd never wanted to leave the City, but now she could barely imagine going back. "It's a big decision," she managed, feeling like she was avoiding something. "I still need to think about it."

* * *

Saffi wiped sweat from her brow with the back of one muddy hand. Planting potatoes was hot work, even with the sun barely risen.

She'd been up at first light, letting out the crocahens to scavenge what they could from the farmyard and the kitchen garden, and she'd almost finished all five rows of potato plants. Plenty to keep the two of them going for the short Felicitean winter. Once she finished this final row, she'd go inside and take Di a cup of tea in bed.

For the first few months, they'd both been up early every day. There'd been a lot to do, especially after they'd had to replant all the fields when the company's shit seeds had failed to germinate and they'd had to start again with their neighbour's help. But lately, Di had been sleeping in a lot more. And, when she did get up, she spent more time in the house than working on the farm.

Not that she even kept the house clean or did much of the cooking – Saffi and Augie had to do those chores between them. Di just seemed to spend the day drifting from room to room and then complaining when she couldn't sleep at night.

Saffi thought Di would sleep much better if she actually left the house and did something, but the one time she'd tried to say anything, she'd nearly had her nose bitten off for her trouble.

With a sigh, she pushed herself to her feet and headed inside. Ten minutes, she thought, and one last try at persuading her to come out and help me with the 'lope fencing. I won't push her. But I wish she would just help me.

* * *

The house was dark when Saffi got back. Augie must have gone out to visit Horse, or shut itself down for the night.

She flicked on the lights and sunk onto the sofa. What did *she* want? That was the question. It had always been about Di— what Di wanted, what made her happy—or about what needed to be done to keep their lives on track. Saffi wasn't sure she could remember the last time she'd done something just because *she* wanted to do it.

A blinking red light caught her eye. A message on their old phone unit. She leaned over and pressed call-back, and the vid-screen flashed into life on the wall.

The call connected and Di appeared, hair wet from the shower. "Saf, babe, there you are. I've been trying to call you all evening. Look at the apartment the company found for us!" She leaned back and gestured at the room behind her. A window took up the whole wall, giving a panoramic view of the city. The furnishings were shiny chrome and bio-couches, and a team of house droids were tidying up, one folding Di's discarded towel and mopping up the water she'd left behind as she raced to the phone.

"Looks... great, love. Really great. I'm glad you like it."

"And you'll never guess who I ran into in the hall," Di gushed. "Tony!"

Saffi shrugged, shaking her head in confusion.

"You remember Tony. From my old job. He's invited us to a party he's having on Saturday and promised to introduce me to some people who are hiring. I could have a job by next week." Di beamed into the camera, eyes sparkling with excitement.

It was always the same, Saffi thought. Di loved everything new, and then the shine wore off.

"I'm sure he knows people in data analysis as well. Or they'll be at the party. Everyone will be there. It'll be easy to find a job for you too once you show your face." Di hadn't seemed to notice Saffi's silence. That wasn't unusual either. Why had she never recognised that before? "So, when are you coming back? I'm sure there's stuff you want to finish off there, but there's only a few weeks until the end of the year. You need to let the company know you're leaving so they can pick you up before it's too late. Why don't you call them in the morning? Then you can be back for the party."

Saffi grimaced, grasping for an answer to the unanswerable

question, wishing Di would just shut up for thirty seconds so that she could think. Images of Augie and Horse, of Seamus and his bevy of clucking brides, of crops glowing in the sunlight, of Ivy and her family, flashed through her mind.

"I'm sorry, love," she said at last. "I think you're on your own this time."

"What?" Di frowned, leaning into the camera. "But you're the one who didn't want to leave the City in the first place!"

"I know." Saffi looked around at the shabby couch, the curtains she'd made for the windows with her own two hands, her dusty boots by the front door. "But, somewhere along the line, this old place became home."

Saffi cut off Di's shocked denial by turning off the screen. It didn't matter, not really. All that was important was still here, with her. She rose and walked through the kitchen, out the back door, and into the moonlight.

Felicity's biggest moon was high in the sky, bright and full. Its smaller companion nestled below it, a sharp crescent. Perhaps Saffi would find a new companion of her own one day but, for now, the moons were enough as they turned her farmyard silver.

A soft crow from the henhouse was Seamus settling to sleep and the 'lopes whuffed from their pen by the barn, dreaming soft herbivore dreams of long grass and sweet water.

Saffi leaned on her garden fence, bare feet nestled in the dirt, and smiled as tears ran down her cheeks. It hurt to lose Di and, more, to lose her dreams of what their future could have been. But this, right here, was where she belonged.

Your Brother's Touchstone

Isabel Lee

Isabel Lee is a writer, artist, and creative technologist from Chicago, Illinois. Her interests include exploring the intersections between code, art, and fiction, and you can find her work online at isabellee.me. She also enjoys painting and watching Korean thriller movies. This is her third published story; previous work can be found in the September 2020 and March 2021 issues of Clarkesworld.

Phillip is about to disappear again. You're a block away from school, and your brother is dragging his feet as you try to pull him across the crosswalk. Your opposite forces cancel out, leaving you at a standstill in the middle of the street. It's a little annoying that he can do this now. He's only eight, fully three years younger and half a foot shorter than you, but taekwondo has really strengthened his resolve this year, while treatment has only weakened yours.

"Noona, I don't wanna goooo," he moans. "School is so stupid. I hate it."

You roll your eyes. "Phillip, it's not a choice." You look around you, at the familiar delis and brick apartments that line the street. You walk these three blocks from Haraboji's townhouse every morning, and lately Phillip has been throwing a fit half the time. An older boy you've seen around before watches with mild interest from the skatepark on the corner of the street, probably wondering if you're going to get run over by a car. "People are looking at us," you hiss at him, but he holds his ground.

"My teacher is so mean," he whines. "She says I don't pay attention, but it's not my fault she's sooo boring." It's only when a car turns the corner that you can finally drag him across the street.

Once you hit the sidewalk, though, he shakes you off and bursts ahead, rounding a corner.

"Phillip, wait!" you call after him, but when you turn the same corner you're greeted by an empty street. You look around you, but there's no crevice he could have hidden in, no alleyway to escape to. He's gone.

You shut your eyes and groan. This is the third time this year that this has happened, and it's not even November yet.

You walk the remaining block to school, joining the steady stream of kids heading inside. You go straight to the Principal's office, where Rosy the secretary is clacking her shiny nails on the keyboard. She raises her eyebrows at you when she sees you walk in. "Good morning, Miss Hana."

"Phillip's sick again," you tell her. She purses her lips slightly, and then just nods and waves you in. Other kids think she's mean, but she's let these absences with Phillip slide. You know it's only because she feels bad for you—maybe she thinks your entire family is ill. You feel her eyes shift to your short, uneven hair, and you quickly murmur a goodbye and escape out the door before she can say another word.

Phillip's absence falls to the background for most of the school day, though during silent reading period you stare at your book, eyes glazing over words, and wonder if he's come back yet. After the final bell rings, you wait for him at the entrance until you realize he's not coming. In fact, he doesn't come back until much later that night.

* * *

"Noona, wake up," a voice whispers into your ear. You open your eyes. In the darkness you can't see much of anything, but you

44

feel his breath on your cheek, hot and quick. You feel a wave of relief, but also a flash of annoyance as you remember your walk home alone. The boy at the skatepark was there again, wearing a beaten red jacket and a weird look on his face the entire time you went down the block.

"Phillip?" you say, lifting yourself up in a daze. You turn on the lamp between your matching twin beds. "Finally, you're back."

"What did you tell Haraboji?" he asks, his eyes wide.

"Huh? I told him you were gonna stay with Mom and Dad tonight."

"Oh." He crinkles his nose. "I hate sleeping in the dry cleaner apartment. It never stops shaking."

"You should be thanking me for covering for you," you say exasperatedly, though secretly you agree. The apartment above your parents' dry cleaners is tiny and boring and hot, not to mention much farther from school. You swing your legs off the bed. "So where did you go this time?"

He thinks for a moment. "A field. It was so huge—I could only see grass. I kept shouting and running and looking for people, but I couldn't find anyone."

You stare at him. "You spent the entire day in a field? Did you eat anything after breakfast?"

He shrugs. "I'm hungry now, Noona."

You walk to the kitchen and turn on the light. From the fridge you dig out leftover kimchi pancake and soup and put them in the microwave. It hums in the background as you scrutinize your brother, who sits at the island with his legs swinging. "Okay, let's go over the clues. Today you were in a field. Last time..."

45

"I was in the woods, somewhere. There was no one there either."
He shivers at the memory. "But the first time this year, I landed
in a street I didn't recognize. I asked a lady for her phone and
tried calling Haraboji and the dry cleaners, but strangers
answered instead."

You punch open the microwave two seconds before it beeps, so
you don't wake up Haraboji. You put the food in front of Phillip
and watch as he scarfs it down quickly. You try to make sense
of the things he's told you, puzzle pieces you can grasp in your
mind but can't quite fit together. The case of your weird, disappearing brother, who eats with his mouth open and has a new
obsession every week, who likes to open and close the door in his
sleep but never remembers doing so the next morning. Who can't
control when he disappears or where he goes. Thinking about it
makes your body tingle all over, a greater mystery than in any of
the detective books that you devour. "You have to learn how to
control this, Phillip," you tell him. "You can't keep disappearing
whenever you feel like it. Rosy is gonna get suspicious."

He pouts. "Noona, I don't know how."

You start to pace, something the people in your books are always
doing. "What's been the same about all the times it's happened?
Were you thinking something, doing something?"

He thinks while chewing. "I don't know... uh, I guess I've always
been outside. And I've always been running, too."

You nod, satisfied. "Okay. Well, we can train tomorrow after my
appointment."

He makes a face at the word *train* but says nothing, finishing the
rest of the food. Then he hops off the chair and heads down the
dark hallway. "G'night, Noona."

You put his plate in the sink and follow him down the hallway, flipping off the light as you leave. Phillip is already out cold when you enter the bedroom, and you tug a little more blanket over him before crashing into your own bed. Whatever he's doing, wherever he's going— all you know is that it's exhausting.

* * *

Haraboji takes you to the hospital after school the next day. He seats himself in the waiting room while you approach the front desk.

"Hi, my name is Hana Chae," you say. "I have an appointment at 4:30?"

"Can I speak to a parent, darling?" the woman drawls from behind the glass, hardly looking up. She mouses around at a massive, ancient computer, reminding you of Rosy.

"They're not here, actually. I came with my grandfather. He doesn't speak English very well," you say, trying to talk as slowly and helpfully as you can. You hate when adults make you repeat yourself, because you weren't 'speaking clearly enough'. "But I know all of my information, so you can just ask me everything."

She looks up at you, and you muster a wide smile. "Alright," she finally grumbles.

After about ten minutes a nurse calls your name. You follow her through the door, past all the regular check-up rooms to the large testing room in the back. She takes your weight and height and swabs your cheek. You tell her how you've felt for the past few weeks, which is fine. Then she withdraws a vial of blood and gives you a pink and white polka-dotted band-aid.

"You're good to go, sweetie," she says. "We'll call Mom and Dad with the results in a bit." Then you walk back to the waiting room where Haraboji has dozed off, gently shake him awake, and head home.

Phillip is sprawled on the floor and shuffling cards when you get back. Playing cards are his current infatuation, and he's been badgering you to play new games all the time. This time, though, you give him a knowing look and he rolls over, disgruntled as he gets to his feet. *I'm going outside*, you say to Haraboji in Korean.

You walk to the backyard, where there's a small meadow that also borders the surrounding houses. Phillip trails behind you. "This is dumb," he announces as you come to a stop amongst the thin grass. This place is little more than a mud pit after it rains, a far cry from the majestic field that Phillip had told you all about yesterday. Still, it's better than nothing.

You point in front of you. "Run. Try to disappear."

Phillip grumbles for a moment, then starts to sprint. He waves his arms around and leaps, then comes crashing down to the ground. He walks back to you. "Nope."

You tell him to try again. You tell him to yell the place he wants to go to before he jumps, to empty his head, to think about flying. You tell him to think about his favorite food, black bean noodles. For half an hour he runs around, with nothing to show for it. The next time he retreats, you're startled to see his eyes glistening. You realize he wants to figure this out just as much as you.

You look at your brother, bruised, dirty, and panting, and hold out your hand. "That's enough for today. Let's go home," you tell him. You help him up and suggest you guys make black bean noodles for dinner. Haraboji only has the instant kind, but still.

Phillip smiles weakly. "And then afterwards we play Spit."

"Yea, okay," you say, even though he beats you every time. Together you start to wade out of the grass, and he never lets go of your hand.

* * *

The weekend comes without any further disappearances. Usually you spend the time with your parents, but today they're doing heavy-duty repairs on the washers and you've been told the dust isn't good for your lungs. Instead, your aunt has volunteered to take you two. Phillip declares he'd rather stay with Haraboji than spend the weekend with a relative he barely knows. You'd honestly prefer the same, but over the phone your mom had insisted you go. *You never see Imo*, she says, which isn't wrong. Aunt Lynne is someone you see solely on Thanksgiving, who hands you a new sweater and then disappears for another year. So on Saturday morning you throw together an overnight bag and grab your library book from the nightstand. Phillip gives you a half-wave from the TV as you walk to the driveway, where her car is waiting.

When you get to Aunt Lynne's apartment and walk through the door, it takes a moment for you to adjust to your surroundings. The place is smaller than both Haraboji's townhouse and your parents' apartment, and filled to the brim with *things*— colorful stained-glass cups, gold-plated bookmarks and silver bangles, a huge tapestry on the wall, gleaming with pale violet and metallic woven threads. You remember the nickname your mom uses for her— *Ggamagui Imo*, Aunt Crow— and it suddenly makes sense.

Your aunt makes small talk with you as you unpack and she boils water for yuzu tea. You tell her about the mystery novel you're currently reading. You can't believe that the main character, only a year or so older than you, is able to take a plane by herself to Monaco, where a billionaire has been murdered. Your mom would never.

Aunt Lynne laughs. Her voice is musical, you think, much brighter than a crow. Like a songbird. "Don't worry, Unni has always been no fun." Her face straightens and you know what she's thinking. "Anyways, Hana, maybe she's right. Flying isn't really safe for you right now."

"But I'm fine," you say quickly. "Nothing has gotten worse for months now."

Aunt Lynne just nods. She takes a big spoonful of yuzu jelly and stirs it into your mug, changing the topic to ask you about school and living with Haraboji. You tell her school is good, that Haraboji is nice but doesn't really care what you do, so you and Phillip have a lot of time to yourself. "We play outside a lot. Phillip was really into jump roping. Now it's cards."

She smiles, and then falls silent. You get the sense that she's hovering over words. "You guys keep yourselves busy, then?" she says softly.

You smile back, uncertain. "I guess."

"And so you know which one of you is the special one, right?" she asks.

You freeze. "What?"

She raises her eyebrows, her eyes glinting. "Well. If you don't know, then it's probably Philip."

You stare at her. Another puzzle piece has suddenly fallen into your lap, it seems. "It is," you say slowly, after a long pause. "He... disappears." Your heart pounds. You and Phillip have guarded this secret your entire life, and speaking it out loud feels monumental, irreversible.

Aunt Lynne's face morphs into something like *Huh, neat.* Something about her reaction flips a switch in you and opens up a floodgate of words. "He's been doing this since he was three, but never more than a few minutes. And no one knows— I've covered for him every time. But now he's disappearing more and more, for hours at a time, sometimes the whole day. And he can't control it. He doesn't know how."

"Phillip just needs to find a touchstone. An emotional anchor," she says simply. "That, and practice."

You mull over this. "Imo, I... how did you even...? Do you...?"

Aunt Lynne shakes her head. "I can't believe Unni never told you. It's probably because she wasn't the special one," she says, smiling. You follow her gaze to the lush tapestry on the wall. "Our family has a way with things, Hana. We see time and space for what it is: fine threads interlocked together, waiting to be pulled and rewoven."

You feel your breath quicken. "So— can you explain why he disappears? What he's actually doing?"

She frowns. "I couldn't tell you. It's different in every generation, every person, even. Phillip will have to figure it out for himself. It's what I had to do."

But he'll have me, you think. You ponder what she said. "Imo... what *can* you do?"

She looks around and her laughter fills the tiny room. "Where do you think I got all of this stuff? Do you think I just bought it?"

* * *

"A touchstone. An emotional anchor," you repeat to Phillip after school. It's a few days later and you're standing in the small backyard meadow again, the sun dipping below the trees.

"What does that even mean?" Phillip asks, his face scrunched. You open your mouth before realizing you don't really know, either.

"Think about something that makes you really happy?" you say. "Or sad. Or excited." Phillip starts spinning around in circles. You cross your arms. "Hey, take this seriously."

"Blah blah blah," he says, stomping around the grass. He's dropped his interest cards since last week and has taken to acting like a dinosaur around the house. After a while of this you turn on your heel and start to head back. You hear Phillip yelp and scurry after you.

When you step through the back door, the sky behind you has darkened to twilight, and to your surprise there are people sitting at Haraboji's kitchen table. They turn around. Phillip crashes into your back as you stand there. "Mom. Dad."

"Hana, come here," your dad says. Your stomach twists. Your parents should be working at the dry cleaners; they shouldn't be here. On the table you see packets of paper, bar charts and paragraphs in thin black ink that look all too familiar.

Phillip untangles himself from your sweater and glances around. "What happened?" he asks. "Why are you guys here?"

Your mom opens her mouth to speak, but your ears close to her words, your head unable to register their meaning. Your world is suddenly wrung, as if it were you that had been spinning.

* * *

Sleeping through the night gets harder now. Your days consist of school and then endless appointments, a blur of different starched hallways and the insides of MRI scanners. At night you lie on your side so that it doesn't feel like you're in a machine. The door opens and closes softly at odd times, every click jolting your body awake. At the umpteenth time you tear off your blankets and yell at the door. "Phillip! Stop it!"

A mound stirs next to you, and you realize it's him. He wasn't near the door at all. But who was? You squint into the darkness, while the blurry form of Phillip's head rears up. "Noona?"

"Sorry, Phillip, I... I had a bad dream," you say. "Go back to sleep."

A few moments pass and he drowsily gets to his feet. You watch him walk to your bed and get under the covers, and you feel the warmth of his small body as he curls up next to you. He hasn't done this in years. "Noona, don't be scared," he whispers.

You lie back down and rest your head on the pillow next to his. His hair has gotten so shaggy and might be just about as long as yours. "You too," you whisper. You close your eyes and try to slow your breathing, in and out and in again until it matches the rhythm of his.

* * *

This is how you remember it happening. You and Phillip are on your way to school on a Monday morning like always. He hasn't had a fit for weeks, ever since that afternoon your parents visited. Today, he busies himself by kicking acorns as you walk down the block, humming the theme song to the ninja cartoon he's always watching. You turn the corner at the skatepark, where the boy

53

you always see is doing ollies on the sidewalk. For the first time Phillip stops to stare at him. "I wanna learn how to skateboard," he announces. The boy is close enough to hear; he looks up and grins.

You look at Phillip, who doesn't smile back. Instead, an expression like you've never seen crosses his face, as if he is totally spooked. He hurries ahead towards the crosswalk, faster than you can keep up. You usually cross the street together, but he dashes across before you reach him. He doesn't see the car yet, but you do. The car doesn't see Phillip yet, but you do.

"PHILLIP!" you scream. The car honks and swerves, and Phillip disappears behind its silver body. For a few awful seconds you stand there in shock. You barely register the car speeding off, leaving behind an empty street. You take a shaky step forward and look up and down the road. You don't see anything, not even Phillip.

The car never hit him. You whisper the words to yourself, willing yourself to believe in them, but doubt creeps into your head as the seconds tick by. He's gone, you know, but is he okay? Is he hurt? The thought of him limping around in an unfamiliar place, unable to leave or get himself help, makes your stomach turn. You stagger back, looking around for anyone who might be able to help.

And then what happens next is something you still can't explain. On the other corner of the street, you see someone gawking at you. In another moment you realize you're staring at Phillip. But his jacket is an unfamiliar color, a bright neon red that envelops his body. His white sketchers are caked in mud. You start to walk to him in a daze, but as soon as you make eye contact he breaks off into a run. In another moment he's gone. You stop in your tracks.

You look behind you, half expecting to see him somehow transported again. But the street's empty, except for a small figure on the other end. The boy at the skatepark watches you from a distance. You start to run towards him, his face apprehensive as you approach. "Have you seen my brother?" you gasp. You know it's a ridiculous question, but you don't know what else to ask. He shakes his head silently.

You feel yourself hyperventilating now. Every other time you've kept your cool, lied through your teeth and played along like your favorite sleuths. But doing so now suddenly seems unfathomable. You want someone to tell you what to do, where to go, how to get him back. All you want is to get him back.

You back away from the skatepark, and your legs move you the remaining block to school. You pass through the front doors and into the Principal's office. Rosy glances up at you as you enter. Your mouth feels dry as you form your words. "Phillip isn't here."

"Sick again?" she asks, raising her eyebrows. She'd probably let it slide a fourth time if you nodded and kept moving. But you shake your head. Her brow furrows. "Then where is he?"

"I don't know," you say, and brace for the world to fall.

* * *

You lie quietly in the half-empty room, listening to voices in the early evening. It's two days later, and Phillip is still missing. After Rosy called your parents, they came and spoke with the officers, and then you all went home. Now your mom and dad switch between shifts at the dry cleaner's so one of them can sit on your bed and stroke your hair. You can hear someone murmuring outside now, see ripples of light leaking in underneath the door.

You remember how the principal and officers had implored you for an explanation, how you had lied. Sitting in that office, you realized there was no possible way to explain everything, especially considering you understood none of it. So you didn't. You told them he ran away. You studied your mom afterwards, but her face was like glass, still and empty.

Now you hear her knocking on the door. "Hana, are you awake? There's—"

"I'm sleeping!" you call immediately, though in reality you haven't slept for more than an hour since Thursday. There's a brief silence, then more murmuring, and the light beneath the door shifts brighter. You press your face into your pillow and shut your eyes.

About an hour passes and you have to go to the bathroom. You creep out of your room. The kitchen is dark; your mom must have left, Haraboji gone to sleep. On your way back, you notice the big white box sitting on the island. There's a card lying on top of it, ornate leaves surrounding a turkey. *Is it Thanksgiving already?* you wonder to yourself, peeking inside. It's hard to make out the scribbling in the darkness, but you recognize the signature at the bottom— Aunt Lynne's annual clothing drop.

Was she out there, a while ago? Is that why your mom had called you? You suck in your cheek, suddenly angry. Unknowingly you had turned away the only person who might have understood what you're going through. Frustrated, you fumble for the light switch and shimmy the lid off the box.

The first thing you lift up is a shawl, undoubtedly her holiday present to you. You hold it up to the light, feeling your breath catch in your chest. The material is nearly identical to the tapestry you had seen on her wall; silver and violet threads weaving into each other, knit tightly into a beautiful fabric. You hold it to your chest, feeling tears sting in your eyes.

You dip your head and blink them away. When you open your eyes, your gaze lands on the other item in the box. It's folded into a neat rectangle, but what you see is undeniably part of a red, puffy jacket. You stare at the bright swath of color, your entire body suddenly very cold and still. You drop the shawl and back away from the table. Your body hits the back door, and before you know it you are slipping outside.

You stumble into the meadow from the backyard, disoriented from lying in darkness all day. Night has fallen and wet grass brushes your ankles, the earth beneath your feet soft from the day's rain. As you stand here, the cool air prickling the back of your neck, you start to bawl. The wall of shock inside you finally succumbs to staggering emotion, the numbness in your chest replaced with sharp pain and confusion. Nothing makes sense to you any more. And your brother is still gone.

You dip your head, trying to catch your breath, and stare at the craters of mud that have risen at the impact of your slippers. *What does it all mean?* You close your eyes and will yourself to remember, to search through every moment. You go back to that morning, see the boy at the skatepark, Phillip's unsettled face, the car flashing by. You see the red jacket. You see his muddy shoes.

You open your eyes. Your body starts to tingle, just like it does when you get to the best part of your books, the part where the teen detective connects all the dots and finds the killer.

Phillip doesn't just disappear.

You wrap your mind around this. You picture Aunt Lynne's gifts, hear her words— *We see time and space for what it is: fine threads interlocked together, waiting to be pulled and rewoven.* Phillip is the special one. He may not be able to see the threads now, but maybe someday he'll learn. You pick up the new puzzle pieces and click them into place, and suddenly you see what you couldn't before: Phillip leaping into the air in this field and arriving at the corner by school: Phillip swallowed in the new red jacket Aunt Lynne got him: Phillip calling strangers when he wanted your family, because those phone numbers once belonged to someone else.

The more you think about this, the more you feel your understanding expand. You remember how much Phillip always denied opening and closing the door at night, though you swear up and down that you had heard him. Is that another Phillip, hovering over your bedroom? How many Phillips have there been? For maybe the first time ever you imagine your brother as a tall and serious grown up. Who does Phillip become? And then you feel your body become very still, because you remember the boy at the skatepark— lanky and silent, but with the same jet black hair, the same restlessness— and you realize you already know.

Phillip comes back, he's not gone, he's okay. He has to be, because he's already here. You chant this to yourself as you close your eyes, a wave of relief passing over your body. You know now why he had reacted the way he did that morning— he must have recognized himself, even when you couldn't. Maybe he understands what he can do now, too. But then you're left with a final mystery: what is this older Phillip coming back for in the first place, over and over? Almost every day you've seen him at the skatepark. Why?

You ponder this for a long time, and the answer creeps up on you slowly. But once you have it, you are sure of its veracity, because it's the only thing that completes the puzzle, the only thing that could make sense. He's coming back to see you. Because wherever and whenever he's from, you aren't there.

This thought echoes in your head for a bit. You're not as alarmed as you wonder you should be. Instead, you feel pulled to action like a magnet, filled with an urgency to do *something*. You tell yourself that you can dwell on all the other implications later, that there are things you have to do in the meantime. After all, Phillip might not know how to get back quite yet. But maybe you can go to him.

* * *

You slip out that morning when Haraboji is just waking up, when he doesn't expect you to wake for hours. You walk quickly through the foggy morning, down the two blocks that take you to the bigger road where you cross the street to school. But today you stop well before and step into the skatepark on the corner. The boy faces away from you on the other side of the pipe, focused on the ground rolling below him. His red jacket is worn, but it fits him now.

Before you approach him, you stop and think to yourself, *It's so early.* You marvel at all the times you remember seeing him here before school, practicing dutifully. He must be so good now. All these times, was he really waiting to catch a glimpse of you? The thought makes you want to cry again, but you steel yourself quickly.

It also occurs to you that today is Sunday, that there's no school to catch you walking to. Briefly, you wonder how he knew to come here this time. It occurs to you that it might be because you'll tell him to, someday. You make a mental note of this.

The boy sees you now, and he starts to cross the pipe to reach you. As he gets closer, you realize how tall he is— taller than Haraboji, taller than Dad. You really look at his face for the first time and realize his eyes are the same as they've always been.

You stare at each other, as if you are both in the presence of ghosts. He shifts the skateboard to his other hand and scratches his head. "Hi, Noona."

"You're here, Phillip," is all you can say. But this isn't your Phillip, not yet. Not ever.

He smiles weakly. "You were always a good detective."

You really do start to cry again now, the words you were going to say next swallowed by your tears. You think he can tell what you would say, though: *You're so big. I'm sorry. I'm so proud of you for figuring out.*

He envelops you into a hug, and you press your face into his jacket in place of words. *You come back*, is what you'd say. And he does. Time and time again.

Revenant

Lisa Short

Lisa Short is a Texas-born, Kansas-bred writer of fantasy, science fiction and horror. She has an honorable discharge from the United States Army, a degree in chemical engineering, and twenty years' experience as a professional engineer. Lisa currently lives in Maryland with her husband, two youngest children, father-in-law and cats. She is a member of the Horror Writers Association and a Futurescapes 2021 alumnus.

Thud. Thud. Thud.

When she was very young, Selina had fallen off the side of a boat, or at least she thought she had—she couldn't quite remember *falling*. But she had been dreaming of the ocean all around her, full of strange, muffled squeaks and groans, and the tarnished, wavering disk of the sun shining through the water, hopelessly out of reach of her outstretched fingers.

Thud. Thud.

She had barely noticed those *thuds* at first; a small part of her memory was filled to overflowing with other intermittent creaks and groans, so many that she couldn't count them up in any meaningful way. *Isn't that the definition of infinity?* she wondered distantly, dreamily, and then—*qualitative only*. That thought was different—colder, stranger.

But the thuds didn't die away, as they always had before. And there was a purposefulness about them—a *deliberation*—Selina was abruptly conscious of a desire to look and see what the source of that thudding was.

Looking. Seeing. It seemed to have been far easier for her to do both at some unknown time point in the past—as though she simply might have wished for it, or flexed a slight muscle of herself, and immediately found fulfillment. Now it was more difficult; great swathes of her awareness were oddly dull, and overtop it all was an unpleasant sensation of immense pressure bearing down upon her. She had no accompanying feelings of suffocation or collapse; she was sure, she and the cool alien flow of thought so intertwined with herself that it *was* herself, that she was in no danger from it. But she didn't like it.

Before she had consciously realized it, she was *seeing* after all. Room after galley after corridor after cluttered mechanical space, all in shades of green and black—she was both surprised and unsurprised, as if part of her had known that this was what she would see but another part had expected—what? Then light blazed up, and Selina recoiled; harsh, gray brilliance poured into one particular room from the corridor just beyond it.

A man lay on his back on the floor of the room, kicking one of the panels lining the walls with both feet. He did so methodically, with measured pauses between each piston-like outthrust of both legs together—*thud!* Then his harsh, sobbing breath, followed by utter stillness, and *thud!* The metal panel shook under the onslaught, then stilled. His rough boots had left smears of unidentifiable filth on the panel's surface, but no other mark, and that cold, distant part of herself told Selina that its integrity was unbreached despite the now hours-long assault launched upon it.

Selina stared down at him. The rest of him was as dirty as his boots, and bloody too—his lip was split, and half an eyebrow was gone in a thick shallow scrape that ran all the way down to his jaw. *Clinic 7*, she thought, or some part of her did. He was in *Clinic 7*, and the corridor beyond was *Emergency Exit 16, intended for ambulatory noncombatants and medical staff only.* But somehow the exit had become an entrance—she couldn't see very far into the corridor, but she had an odd sensation of relief through it, from the grinding pressure bearing down on every other part of her.

Thud!

"Stop!" she cried involuntarily. He froze, legs drawn back, and Selina froze, too, at the terrible grating noise that had emerged from herself, barely comprehensible as a word. She tried to clear her throat, then to swallow, and found that she could do neither. She tried again, reflexively, and *something* happened—a small shift, somewhere, and when she spoke again, a voice far more recognizable as her own echoed from the wall speaker high above the man's head. "Who are you?"

He jerked up onto his elbows and scrabbled backwards until he fetched up against the wall opposite the panel, the back of his head smacking into it with an audible thump, and Selina listened in blank dismay to the spate of gibberish that erupted from his mouth. It wasn't English—was it? She tried matching it against all the other languages she (or at least, that icy, subtle presence that was also herself) knew. It was more like English than it was anything else, except that it was indisputably *not* English.

She realized, after a second incomprehensible flood of syllables had erupted from him, that it was the sharp, barking sounds he made regularly mid-speech that were befuddling her: *glottal stops*, her other self informed her coolly. She found she was able to filter them out and replace them with the consonants they had once clearly been, and then at least try to fit her own speech into a form he could understand. "Stop," Selina repeated, more temperately. "Who are you? What are you doing here?"

"I," he said, and choked on a sob. "I'm Aylen Bells Laren. Son of Bells Laren Mord, Bells daughter of Laren Mord Pers and—"

"Aylen?"

"Yes." He shut his mouth tightly on that syllable, which had survived the language shift untouched.

"But what are you doing here?" She paused. "You shouldn't be here." Her voice sounded uncertain, even to herself. He *shouldn't* be here. She was sure of that, in a bone-deep and unshakeable way. Yet he *was* here—was she supposed to prevent that? Or remedy it, as it had already occurred? Her cold and distant thought-companion had no answer to that. Its absence left her feeling strangely unbalanced.

"My people are dying," said Aylen. "My *family* is dying." He sat up, then lurched to his feet. "We left generations ago, my ancestors, just as your ancestors told us to do. We haven't come back—we've stayed in the Wastes, where we belong." He lowered his head when he said the last part, his tone oddly servile—but his eyes gleamed beneath the narrowed slits of their heavy lids, and a muscle jerked in his jaw. "Only I came here—only I. I thought—a few others have tried, though not in my generation or my mother's. My mother's mother was one who tried, she and a group of others—she alone made it back, across the Wastes, and said that there was no way in, anymore—the Enclave was sealed—"

The Enclave. *Home.* Yes, that felt right—*yes,* said her icy other self. *We are the Enclave.*

Aylen was still speaking— "But when I came, on the third day the earth shook—it shook, and shook, and something struck me in the head. When I awoke, it was nearly sunset, but I saw that a passage had opened, a passage in the earth itself, leading—*down.*" His eyes and mouth were stretched wide with remembered wonder and terror. "It was full of dirt and rocks; it took me even more days to clear it away. But I thought, maybe you—someone— might be sorry, that your people hadn't helped us before, I thought—" He stopped, hugging himself tightly, then straightened his spine and lifted his head up to stare directly at the wall speaker. "I ask you to help us now. Or *I* can help *you*—" The words began to tumble out of him, faster and faster. "I can, I can bring you whatever you want, from outside, you don't go outside, do you? Or—"

"Wait," said Selina distractedly. He was immediately silent once more, motionless except for the faint shudders he couldn't seem to control—*fatigue*, her thoughts suggested. *Hunger. Exhaustion.*

My family is dying.

"Of what?" He stared blankly up at the wall. "What is your family dying of?"

"The disease. The one that comes with the dust storms, in the Wastes." He said *disease* as if it were *Disease*, as though there were only one of any importance. "When our ancestors tried to return here to escape from it, your ancestors drove them away." His hands had curled into fists at his sides.

What Disease? Selina demanded of herself, but again her inner voice, the one that knew so much and felt so little, was silent. But memory stirred—the pure, thin red light of *deflection lasers* for destroying any debris that might block the solar panels or damage the external ventilation machinery. She had seen them firing, cutting through a dust-choked haze with a clear, vivid beauty against a sky sapphire with dusk, streaked with crimson-edged clouds—and the faint, far-off sounds of high-pitched, anguished screams—

Animals, whispered that cool inner voice. *The lasers were also intended to ward off any wildlife incursions, to protect the Enclave. The Enclave must not be overrun.*

Did animals scream when they died?

"Speak," she said aloud, curtly. "Tell me what the symptoms are, of your *Disease.*" He didn't know what *symptoms* were, she could see that clearly enough, but he was certainly willing to talk about the Disease. He seemed to get angrier and angrier as he spoke, his language descending into graphic convulsions of ruin—vomiting, purging, cannibalistic madness and finally, death—

"Enough," Selina said abruptly. He had lost some of his terror of her, or gained courage from his self-catalyzing rage, and trailed off rather than snapping into obedient silence. *Be of use,* she thought angrily at that vast, cold part of herself. *What could this Disease be? Analyze it!*

The results of that analysis took only a minute or two; she eagerly turned her attention to them, then sagged in disappointment. She had found over twenty different diseases, not just one *Disease,* that matched a statistically significant majority of his lurid description. She flipped rapidly through the tabulated results, calming as she realized that they *did* all have certain similarities—*my medical stores,* she thought with an odd and unfamiliar reluctance. *My medical stores have antiparasitics.* The Disease was almost certainly caused by parasites. *But the stores—!* The reluctance was from that other part of herself, passionless but rigid in its disinclination to allow access to them.

He will bring back more people, it insisted. *They will overrun the Enclave. We must not*—and abruptly she was overwhelmed with a torrent of schematics flashing past her consciousness, great dead bands of energy grids covered by uncounted years of dirt and debris. *We must not*—the deflection lasers, and the screaming—

A spasm shook her and a wall panel, not the one Aylen had been kicking, grated open. He stumbled over to it and fell to his knees, clawing at the torrent of vials spilling onto the floor. "Add enough water each to fill the vial, recap it and shake it as hard as you can," Selina whispered—whispered because quite a bit of herself was fighting speech now and that was all she could squeeze past it. "The water must be clean. Distilled." He stopped grabbing at the vials to stare up at her uncomprehendingly. "*Boiled*, then. One vial per person about your size. Less or more if different." Her speech was fragmenting back into the hoarse, grating whine of her first attempt.

Aylen's hands, half-hidden under the vials, suddenly stilled. His eyes squeezed shut and his mouth sagged open; a torrent of new tears welled up from beneath his closed lids, sliding like quicksilver down the tracks already dried in dirt and blood. Then his head snapped up, his glistening stare fixed on the wall speaker; the muscles under his flesh shifted, and his face looked years older than it had before, rigid with despair. "It doesn't matter," he said harshly. "It doesn't matter if it's poison instead of medicine. We're dying anyway." He scooped up the last of the vials into the pouch he'd made of the bottom of his ragged tunic, then pushed himself back up onto his feet and across the room to where the exit corridor gaped open.

"Wait!" She could barely force out the single word. *"Wait."* She wrestled for control of her voice and was briefly triumphant. "If you think it might be poison, why did you come here at all?"

She thought he would ignore her, and just break and run—the muscles along the backs of his arms and legs tensed, and she had no way to stop him. But he paused, and turned his head, though not enough to face her completely once more. "My people have a story," he said slowly. "A legend. Do you want to hear it?"

Yes. No. Her other self was the dissenter, though strangely muffled—something about *irreparable damage to the central processing unit with unstructured memory upload*—Selina tried desperately to say both at once, but all that emerged was a burst of static. Aylen shuddered, then took a deep breath.

"Once," he said, only a little unsteadily, "many, many generations ago, the land wasn't like it is now—there were no Wastes, no dust storms, only rolling green hills and blue skies and the people were content. *Most* of the people were content—but there were a few that were afraid, for they saw the seeds being sown of what would come, that most of the land would die in a Great Devastation, though quickly or slowly they weren't sure.

"So those few gathered up as many as they could find who believed, or could be convinced to believe, the way they did, and they built the Enclave. They hid it deep in the mountains, for they knew that after the Devastation, many others, too many, might try to find them and take what they had worked so hard to build, to save themselves.

"The Enclave was a marvelous place, powered by the Sun itself, able to feed and shelter an unimaginable number of people...and ruled, *not* by people, for they'd proven to be too fickle, too selfish, but by a *Machine*, a vast and unliving mind able to carry on a thousand tasks at once, a mind that never allowed itself to be swayed in judgement by any one person's desires nor even any desires of its own.

"But then...the Machine became corrupted."

Memory, as if it had been beating against a seawall of her other self's will until just that moment, broke over her in an agonizing torrent—not just her own memories, bright explosions of light and heat and sensation sharp as a hundred knives, but her other self's memories too, the *thrum of the Enclave's very lifeblood churning down, down* until the deep silence filled all its mechanical spaces.

THE BULKHEAD DOORS ARE CLOSING!

Those monstrous, impervious doors, designed all too well to lock out even the air of the outside world, had sealed themselves shut, massive hydraulics sparking and fusing as the Enclave's AI was ravaged by an electronic virus that had somehow eluded all their security measures. Several thousand of the Enclave's residents had managed to escape through the emergency exits, out of the tomb the Enclave was rapidly becoming, until the virus had found those too.

Aylen's voice rose. "And then the Enclave's people began to die as well. But one man knew how to save them all. One man knew how the Machine could be cleansed of its corruption—that the Machine could be *remade*, in the likeness of a living person."

One man. One *face*. That memory burned like acid, every detail so crystal clear in her mind's eye that its owner might have been standing right there next to Aylen in the clinic, smiling up at her (smiling *down*, he had always smiled *down* at her, he had been so tall, they had all teased him about his great and gangling height)—

Sitaram.

Sitaram and his mice and his *rapid neural biomapping*—it had been his side project, his personal obsession. The year before the virus came, he'd managed to map lab mice, one cortical layer at a time, in a matter of mere hours instead of the years that the painstaking manual coding from scratch that the construction of a semi-autonomous machine AI required. But the mapping process had invariably killed the mice, and their newly birthed neural networks had sparkled and died along with them.

Then Sitaram had tried freezing the mice first, live, so quickly that their body cells had had no time to rupture. To the marvel (and deep disquiet) of everyone else, the resulting tiny, intricate murine networks had thrived for months, still attached to their deep-frozen donors.

Those little networks hadn't been able to actually *do* much, though; they had been only mice, after all.

Aylen sucked in a deep, shuddering breath. "But that person would have to die, so that all the Enclave could live again."

Sitting in the dark with Sitaram, after they'd turned off all the lights to stretch what was left of the backup generator fuel. Sitaram's face lit from beneath by the faint glow of the portable CO_2 monitor, the numbers on the display creeping slowly, slowly up and up.

I know how to turn the machines back on, Ram.

The tear tracks on his cheeks reflecting the monitor's status markers in yellow and red, the pinpoints of light shining like fireflies in his wet dark eyes. Her own arm, pale and freckled, extended toward the syringe squeezed too tightly in his white-knuckled fist.

Am I dead? Selina screamed at her other self. *Am I dead—am I*—and suddenly she saw a room, or what was left of a room, ugly and jagged in the harsh green-and-black of a night vision camera. For a long moment she couldn't understand what she was seeing. The objects that filled the room were lumpy, irregular but still bizarrely angular—then she realized she was looking at *ice*. The maze of pipes filling the room, leading to the coffin-sized tank in its center, had become fantastical crystalline sculptures of whatever scraps of ambient humidity had slowly leached into the room through its seals. Those pipes, still somehow holding pressure after all those years, all those *centuries, or even longer?* full of frigid liquid helium—the *tank*, holding—

"I told my family I thought there might still be people in the Enclave who could help us." Aylen laughed, a harsh humorless bark. "But there's only the Machine left, after all." Then he did run, his legs visibly shaking as they carried him out of her limited sight, into the grayish haze emanating from the far unseen end of the corridor.

She must have restarted the ventilation machinery, just as she had promised Ram she would. There were hundreds of thousands of hours of audiovisual object memories in her tables, far more than the brief handful of years she had spent as Selina, *only* Selina living in the Enclave. People in the Enclave's rooms and galleys and corridors, laughing and crying and eating and sleeping and fighting and making love—

But the rooms, the galleys, the corridors were all empty now, lightless voids. Even the mice were gone.

"Where did they all go?" Selina tried to shout after him. "All the people left alive, still inside the Enclave, *where did they all go?*" But her voice was only a broken, useless stutter from the wall speaker, and Aylen was already gone.

I thought you might be sorry, that you hadn't helped us before.

I thought there might still be people here who could help us.

But there's only the Machine left, after all.

A sharp sense of heat, of warning, touched Selina's conscious-ness. *Power expenditure in excess of current storage capacity,* whispered the cold indifference of her other self. *Initiating shutdown.*

Selina was running along the boat's edge, her mother's voice echoing in her ears—*don't run, you'll slip and fall, Selina!*—and her foot hit a puddle and skidded forward so abruptly she didn't even have time to scream before she tumbled over the side. A brief, gut-wrenching sensation of weightlessness and then she hit the water. It was shockingly cold, enveloping her all around and far, far over her head in a rushing roar of bubbles, but there was nothing for her desperately clawing hands to grab onto. Selina lifted her head, eyes burning in the salt, as the rippling silver orb of the sun receded further and further from her out-stretched fingers.

Dashing, Through the Spaceship

Anna Martino

Brazilian SFF writer and editor,
publishing both in English and
Portuguese — expect to find British
spelling and a Latino sense of
humour... You can find my work at
annamartino.com.

"Commander Silva wants *what*, sir?"

"A dog, Martedi. She wants to pet a dog. Come on, it's not that hard. Canis familiar: four limbs and a cold wet nose, with a tail connected to its back... Honestly, you hot-house kids! Don't they teach you anything useful in those compounds? Anyway, it's the Commander's last wish, and upon my honour..."

"Drop the dramatics, Camargue! She didn't ask for the blood of her enemies laced with gin," said Lieutenant Costa with a long sigh that made the poor ensign cringe. When the enrolment officer told Martedi that a spaceship crew was like a family, they forgot to mention that the lieutenants would fill the role of the bickering siblings looking to establish their position at the pecking order.

And now the bickering siblings had an unlikely problem in their hands. If Commander Silva had asked for the blood of her adversaries, she'd have it in fanciful glasses within the hour. But a dog?

"Ensign Martedi, contact the nearest base and see if they know anyone with a licence for such animals... You'll have better luck trying a zoo or a Living History reservation, try those first." Camargue then turned to Costa. "Did the Commander ask for a specific breed?"

"There are different breeds?"

"Martedi, don't interrupt me!" Costa stifled a nervous laughter, and Camargue then turned to her, cold as the outside air. "You should supervise the quest since you find it such a laughable matter. And you might as well pick the animal yourself, or else the ensign will end up bringing a cow abroad!"

"A what now?" Martedi made the mistake of asking, and had to run away from the room before Camargue cuffed his ears as he shouted a fine selection of descriptions about the ensign's birthplace, mental capacities and upbringing, and while Costa choked on her laughter.

* * *

After a couple of hours studying the subject in question, Ensign Martedi concluded people from the First Generation were soft in the head. A "dog" was too broad a term: there were different shapes, sizes, colours and uses for that pre-space age creature. How was he supposed to know that?

But the Space Fleet didn't pay him to think about his lacklustre education or the minutiae of such bygone beasts; he had received an order and had to go through with it, however absurd it sounded. "I found a Living History community who owns this dog thing, ma'am," he informed Lieutenant Costa later that day. "They breed the specimen for such purposes. Bereavement animals, they call it. They said we're welcome to borrow it."

"Oh, excellent, fantastic." Another long sigh from Costa. It reminded Martedi of his mother whenever someone from the family came with more news from the battles over the settlement borders. "I'll inform Camargue and get to the reservation as soon as possible. Time is of the essence."

"Ma'am…" Martedi hesitated. "Permission to speak?" Costa nodded as she stood up, the creaking of her joints and the creaking of the chair making a duet. "I was told the Fleet will promote Lieutenant Camargue to Commander when…"

"When this is over?" Costa helped Martedi, and the ensign nodded, relieved. "Well, he is the eldest of the lieutenants, so I suppose they will pick him up for the duty. Why are you asking?"

"The place will have a new atmosphere once he becomes the boss."

That was the understatement of the millennium, cocooned in politeness and professional distance. Commander Silva was one of the last members of the First Generation, the last of the space pioneers. She was passion incarnate. Camargue and Costa belonged to the Second Generation, born to parents who lived in the days before the space conquest. Costa had been born on Earth, while Camargue belonged to a Mars base—as much of a hot-house human as Martedi, but with enough first hand memories of the "good old days" back on Earth.

But regardless of their birthplace, the fact was that the grand age of discoveries was past them—what need was there for the curiosity that moved humanity across the galaxy, now that the hard work had finished?

"Don't you like Lieutenant Camargue?"

"I reckon it'd be a better question to check whether he likes me, ma'am."

"I suppose he could do with a smart ensign, so do your best to keep him pleased. Now, tell me about the dog. Does it have a name?"

"It's a Canis familiaris of the Teckel variety, ma'am, about three years old. It has a dark coat and knows how to deal with children and elders."

"Martedi, that's not what I asked," Costa sighed, pinching the bridge of her large nose. "Never mind. I'll inform Camargue you found it. The sooner we do this... Well, the sooner it ends."

Because it had to end. It wasn't what Lieutenant Costa wanted, Martedi could tell from the weathered look in her hooded eyes. But the Fleet wasn't paying for her opinions either, so she soldiered on, hoping to be transferred to another spaceship or another planet as soon as possible.

But those thoughts were as useful as a raincoat on Mars. It'd be for the best to look towards that Teckel variety, whatever it was.

*　*　*

The Teckel variety was the oddest thing Martedi has ever seen in all of his nineteen years.

It was ridiculously shaped, for starters: built like a small oxygen tank laid on its side, with woefully short legs and ears that were just too long. Its bark was too deep for such a compact animal, and again the ensign wondered why his Commander would want to stroke the fur of such a wild thing as her last wish.

Costa, on the other hand, was besotted. "Oh, what a pretty boy!" she smiled upon seeing the specimen in the arms of the Living History reservation manager. It was the first proper smile she gave in over two months.

Martedi tried not to laugh at the manager's historical jogging trousers and ceremonial hoodie, and bit his tongue so not to pass comment on the ridiculous houses in the walled community. Those reproductions of 21st architecture were too huge and too beige, so different to the squat, silver-panelled lodges of his childhood.

"Yes, a bonny creature," said the manager as he scratched the specimen's head. "A little heartbreaker, our Dashing is. Everyone's favourite. I am sure he will make your Commander happy in her last moments."

"I can only hope so. And what a darling you are," Costa bowed down to caress the specimen's black fur. "Yes, you're a splendid boy, aren't you? You are! It's been so long since I saw one of those. Brings back memories..."

"You had a Daschund back home, Lieutenant?"

"She was fifty percent Daschund and fifty percent God knows what. Clone of a clone, my dad's inheritance pet from the days when he lived on Earth. She didn't look this good, though."

"We breed them in the old-fashioned way over here. Our Doxies are all one of a kind," the manager sounded like a proud father. And while he talked, the specimen wiggled from its grizzly caretaker's arms and dashed straight to Martedi, who froze on the spot. Though the animal was little, it had sharp teeth—a bite on the right spot and Martedi could bleed half to death. He had researched that sort of thing. "Just... Just what is it doing?"

"Why, he's sniffing you," the manager smiled. "That's his way to make friends. Come back here, Dashing, you're frightening the poor officer!"

Martedi wanted to argue that he had seen many battles before he had joined the fleet—he had grown up in a Martian frontier outpost, after all: blood and guts by the red roads were common occurrences. A hairy cylinder with dysfunctional legs would not frighten him.

But he kept quiet for the sake of his pride, if not because he didn't want the reservation manager to think ill of the Fleet. And all for the better, because Lieutenant Costa began discussing the logistics with the manager as she held the specimen close to her chest as if it was a long-lost toy.

* * *

"Only one caretaker aboard, ma'am? Is that enough to contain that beast?"

"We're dealing with a dog, lad. We're not bringing a lion to the spaceship," Costa said as they rode past the gardens towards their ship.

"Is that as dangerous as a dog?"

"Martedi, please tell me you are joking." The ensign, however, didn't dare to open his mouth again, flushed red with embarrassment. "Didn't they teach about the animals of Earth back at school?"

"Why would they? It's not like any of us compound kids would ever end up there, anyroad. And if any of us ever ended up there, what would be the chances of actually meeting those creatures?" Martedi straightened up his shoulders, checking and adjusting his position. If he carried on running his mouth when nervous, he'd never be promoted. "If you allow me to speak, ma'am."

"Permission granted, lad. What did your family have, back in your hometown? Just wondering."

"They had what everyone had, ma'am. A plot of land and a job building the roads."

"But no pets."

"No pets, no. There was no food or air or time for such..." "For such fancies," he was going to say. But you couldn't say those things out loud to a superior—not if you planned to stay on the ship. He attempted to remember that the mission wasn't about him or his upbringing, or about the superior breeding of Lieutenant Costa—even though he'd never imagine she was this rich, with parents that could keep cloned souvenirs from Earth.

That errand was about Commander Silva—who probably grew up in houses like those in the Living History area, and wore clothes such as those weird jogging trousers and ceremonial hoodies in her youth. She had been born with her feet on a different ground, with a sky that wasn't rusty but an odd shade of washed blue.

Martedi didn't know whether he should envy his commander's peaceful and bountiful past, or to be disgusted by that silly display of wealth and pride. The little beast was superfluous, yes, but blameless—a token of the past, that was all.

* * *

Martedi expected the dog handler to be older—or, at least, to look like they knew what they were doing. The caretaker, however, was only a couple of years older than he was, dressed up in the reservation flannel and denim work garb, wearing long braids on her jet-black hair.

"I come from a family of dog breeders, if that's what you are wondering," said the young handler, seeing Martedi's doubtful look. "But don't you worry, Dash here knows better than to cause trouble."

"It's not the animal I'm worried about, to be honest."

"Is it your first death ceremony? I suppose people over here go through this fast. I mean, she's top brass, the Fleet won't skimp on the painkillers. It'll be over sooner than you'll know."

"Small mercies," he whispered to himself, as Dashing approached to sniff his boots. "Is this really necessary?"

"Dash's not gonna bite you, silly lad. He thinks you're friendly. So, you've been here for long?"

"Three years", Martedi said as he tried to keep composed.

"Why, you signed up young! Space sailor's life the one for you, then? Or were you voluntold?"

"It was either this or road building, and I didn't want road building. What about you? Always wanted to breed these beasts?"

"Dashing is a *dog*, not a *beast*. And yes, I am to the manner born, to quote the scripture."

"Martedi! Where is the damn animal?" Lieutenant Camargue, in his dark blue dress uniform, marched inside the docking bay in a hurry. He looked every inch the heir apparent, from his slicked, parted slate grey hair to the tips of his well-polished boots. Upon seeing the young handler, Camargue lowered his voice. "You must be Pereira. Welcome aboard. So, is the animal ready?" The young girl, tongue-tied by that demonstration of anger and power, only nodded. "Have it properly leashed at all times. It's my ship, and I don't want a mess. I understand the creature is not to be kept on artificial gravity for long, is that correct?"

"It does a number on his poor joints, yes" the handler said, in a futile attempt at regaining her former composure.

"Then we shall not tarry. Come along," he signalled they should follow him down the ash coloured corridors.

Of course, the crew had to stop to watch the strange procession. Many, like Martedi, have never seen a dog that close before or ever, and only held back from making questions about the beast because of Camargue's imposing presence at the head of the queue. While registering the childlike wonder and curiosity in his friends, the ensign also noted some of his colleagues couldn't disguise a different breed of smile—they weren't curious about the dog; they were disgusted at the display of such an Earthly vanity, unfit for the time and the place.

Lieutenant Costa, meanwhile, was waiting by the door of the Commander's cabin. She lowered herself to pat the dog and Dashing almost jumped on her with unalloyed joy, looking for safety in her arms. "Come on, Dashing," Costa smiled one more time. "You have a big job, now."

"Please refrain from speaking to the animal as if it could understand things," Camargue sighed. "It's unbecoming."

"When you get the promotion, you can issue orders. Until then, shut the deuce up," Costa replied, almost baring her teeth like the dog. The grimace only lasted for a second, but it burned on Martedi's mind for all time.

* * *

In the end, it was all too peaceful: Commander Silva passed away with her first officers around her instead of a family, holding on to Dashing as she lost consciousness in the same way one falls asleep. Contrary to what Martedi expected, there were no deathbed speeches, no anointment of the next commander. Silva was tired of all that ceremony, and the one thing that brought her joy was the dog snuggled on her lap.

Martedi paid attention to Costa's heartfelt tears, the way

Camargue's hands betrayed his contained impatience and how the younger officers wanted the whole thing to end so they could go on with their work. But the one thing that jarred him was how the commander died with a smile on her lips. Martedi couldn't remember his own parents smiling in that way, or the friends he had lost in the skirmishes at the frontier.

No wonder his shipmates were rolling their eyes: who among them had known such a sedated death in their families?

Costa murmured something about God taking care of Commander Silva's soul; Camargue sighed and closed his eyes during the prayer, but he was the first to raise his head once Costa ended the litany. "There, it's finished. Remove the dog, please, and let us proceed with the rest of the affair."

"Could you please give us a moment?" Costa complained.

"We've had the moment. Life goes on, and so should this ship. Martedi, on your feet, lad—take the handler and the dog somewhere they can rest. As for us," he turned to the officers, "let us carry on as our former commander would expect us to."

But the tears still ran from Costa's face as she picked up the dog and left the room, followed by the other officers. Martedi was the last to leave—mesmerized by the raucous, undiluted sadness and weariness and the deep smugness in Lieutenant Camargue's eyes as he looked around the room that would soon be his.

* * *

"How bad is it, this news?"

"It's not bad, Miss Pereira. Unexpected, perhaps, but not bad."

"Back at my patch of land, 'unexpected' almost always means trouble."

In Martedi's patch of space too, only he'd never admit it out loud. It wasn't bad news, he repeated to himself over and over, and yet, the nasty feeling in his stomach was still here, making him queasy.

They'd followed all the rules and protocols of the Fleet: the communication officer transmitted the death announcement to the other spaceships in a timely fashion, neither too soon as not to appear too eager, nor too late as if they had to hide an unnatural death; Silva's body was prepared and then sent away for incineration with all the expected pomp.

The one thing out of order was that the Fleet made Lt. Costa Commander of the spaceship at the end of the daily cycle. It wasn't the news that made Martedi queasy, it was the way the Fleet announced their decision. "'Though he is the oldest lieutenant, the Fleet does not believe Lt. Camargue is ready for such an onerous duty such as the command of such an important spaceship'," Martedi read out loud the Fleet message to Miss Pereira. "Wait, there's more. 'This was the explicit recommendation of Commander Silva, and we will acquiesce to her sound advice.'"

"Well, are you happy with your new commander?" Pereira asked as Martedi prepared the dispatch ship. Dashing left the handler's arms and trotted to sniff Martedi's arm and hands. "You may have your own opinions, you know."

"Not when I'm in uniform and aboard a spaceship," Martedi stiffened and then laughed when the specimen's cold nose touched the palm of his hand. "Hey, you. Stop it!"

"Why don't you stroke Dashing's ears? Here, try this." Pereira guided Martedi's hands over Dashing's cranium. The mixture of fur and cartilage and warmth felt odd to the ensign, just like the puff of hot air coming from the animal's nostrils or the bumps and callouses in Pereira's hand guiding his movements.

There, then: that was what his former Commander was looking for to guide her through the fear as she died. It was comfortable and joyful, though fleeting as vapour. How great it must have been to have received that sort of caress when your child, instead of the harrowing uncertainty of the red roads of his youth, where the silence was an enemy as dangerous as the ray guns.

"Ensign Martedi!"

It was Lieutenant Camargue, still in his pristine dress uniform. Martedi removed his hand from Dashing as he stood up. The lieutenant's face was as placid as always, his voice as bossy as it had always been, and yet he looked different. Was it the lock of hair falling over his forehead, almost touching the eyelid? Or the way he looked over the dock before entering the place, surveying exits and entrances like a seasoned soldier about to enter an ambush?

"I will escort the lady back to the reservation myself," Camargue said to the ensign. "I suppose it is the least I can do to thank them for their kindness. Please prepare the transportation."

Though it was odd that a lieutenant would perform such a minor task, Martedi wouldn't bother to contest the order. What stopped the ensign on his tracks was the fact the lieutenant had said "please".

In the split second between hearing Camargue's words and replying 'yes, sir', Dashing escaped from Miss Pereira's hands and, true to its name, dashed through the door and into the main corridor leading to the bridge.

Pereira and Martedi ran after the dog, who was barking as if trying to send a distress call to all and sundry in the galaxy. People screamed at the scene; half the security guards thought the ship was under attack and the other half joined the mad chase, trying to get the dog before he caused a disaster.

Dashing knew where he was going—even if it took him several rounds to divert from the humans stopping him from arriving at Commander Costa's cabin, scratching the door as he yelped in an anguished cry.

Martedi saw the body before he could comprehend what had happened in the darkened cabin. The small pool under Commander Costa's laid-down body looked as placid as the surface of a Martian lake. Silence in the untouched room, the same sort of silence after an attack at the frontier outposts: time to come out of the foxholes and comb through the debris.

It was Pereira's scream that put two and two together. Dashing jumped towards Costa's lap, trying to rouse her up. Someone in the corridor screamed an auxiliary ship had left the dock. And Martedi, between duty and the dog, decided he'd help the dog, and ran towards Costa to help revive her.

* * *

Martedi later told Costa and the Fleet representatives about how the failed insurrection went about. And he made a point of informing the officials of Dashing's role in the affair. "If it weren't for him, perhaps we'd have found Commander Costa too late."

"Saved by a hairy cylinder with small legs. You don't get to say this a lot these days," Commander Costa smiled for the briefest of moments. "The Fleet will promote you, Ensign. You showed great courage in the aftermath."

"Thanks, ma'am, but I've decided I'm staying over here for the time being."

"Over here" was the Living History reservation. He had escorted Miss Pereira and Dashing back to the beige houses after the commotion died down and the insurrection ringleaders disposed of. And, on the spur of the moment, he decided that if the museum could employ a hot-house kid who had never owned a pet, he'd more than gladly take the position.

"Did that man plan to blame poor Dashing for the riot?" Pereira asked.

"No, I don't think he expected Dashing to foil his plans. He was too Earthly, in that aspect" Martedi looked to Dashing asleep on its bed by the corner of the room. Everything was beige in there, save for Dashing's dark fur, the brick red bed, and Pereira's red flannel shirt. "I suppose they didn't teach Second Generation officers how to improvise in the Fleet."

"But they taught you?" Commander Costa tried to sound nonchalant, but she couldn't help sounding offended. Though Camargue tried to kill her, they shared the same education that Martedi now mocked.

"I grew up in a Martian frontier under heavy dispute, ma'am," Martedi shrugged. "If you don't move, you end up dead."

By the way Costa frowned, Martedi guessed it was the wrong thing to say. She didn't move when Camargue invaded her living quarters demanding explanations about the promotion, and that was why she ended up head first against her own working table. Martedi didn't retract his words, however. Costa had to learn how to move if she wanted to have a peaceful death. There would always be someone bigger wanting her place, after all.

"Suppose he took us with him," Pereira asked as she drank from a flask. "The two of us and Dashing. What then?"

"We'd be dead by now. No manoeuvres and no mercy for expendable people," Martedi looked to Dashing as it snored. "Are they all like this?"

"Like what?"

"Calm in their sleep." Martedi took a sip of the flask. Whatever was inside, it burned his throat and made him cough. Dashing woke up and raised its head in the sound's direction, looking for the ensign to make sure he didn't need help.

In the end, all Martedi felt was pity—for Commander Silva's longing and Commander Costa's awakening, and for the former Lieutenant Camargue's fall from grace. But Martedi refused to feel pity for himself. He didn't know what the future would turn out to be, but now was a good a place as any to start. "Rest easy, Dash," he smiled. "I suppose we are not going anywhere just yet."

The Keeper

Susan E. Rogers

Susan Rogers lives in St. Pete Beach, Florida, retired from a Social Work career in Massachusetts. Retirement was the catalyst for her life-long ambition to write. Her other interests include genealogy and psychic spirituality, often twisting these into her writing. She self-published her first book in 2018 about her own psychic experiences. Since 2020, she has had short fiction published in anthologies and several literary magazines.

Bridget scrunched up her chubby nose as she pushed open the door to his room and waited for the creak she knew would follow. She walked on the exaggerated tiptoes of a four-year-old until she reached the big chair. Then she waited. It wouldn't be long until the bleary blue eyes would welcome her. She never looked away from the old man slumped in the overstuffed chair, the green fabric worn to shiny threads on the arms. She listened to the raspy wheeze that puffed past his lips.

The eyes snapped open and this was her cue. She climbed onto his bony lap and settled in. A tangy smell of shaving cream clung to his cheeks, mixed with the sweet aroma of the peppermint candy that perpetually tumbled around his mouth. The gray sweater was furry-soft against her arms. Spindly fingers gently brushed the wayward auburn curls from her forehead. He whispered a tale to her in a strange tongue. Her plump mouth moved almost imperceptibly, mimicking his words, until she slept in the cot of his arms.

* * *

"It makes me nervous." Annie lifted her hand holding the knife and brushed an unruly ginger curl from her eyes. She dropped the peeled potato into the pan on the table. "Twelve grandchildren and sixteen other great-grandchildren. Not one of them will go near him." A slight breeze blew across the screened porch and mussed her hair again. "Nobody even calls him grandfather; he's always *The Old Man*. If I were Maureen I wouldn't let Bridget go anywhere near him. God forgive me, he's my grandfather but he gives me the creeps."

The older woman stopped peeling the potato she held and looked at her daughter. "Ownie wouldn't hurt her – or anybody." She pursed her lips. "He never has. He's always been gentle despite himself. You shouldn't say those things, Annie."

"Maybe not, but you can't tell me you don't feel it too." Annie grabbed another potato from the basket. "I've seen the look on your face when he calls and you have to go into that room." She waved the knife in her mother's direction. "And he's never paid any attention to any of the other kids, only Bridget." She pitched the peeled potato into the pot for emphasis.

"I don't know why, either. Maybe because she's the youngest. He knows he doesn't have much time left. He's ninety-three after all." Mary sighed and remembered the man her father had been in his younger years. He never was one to show affection to his children, no hugs or kisses for sure. Paddy and Tom left home as soon as they could find a way to keep themselves, their way of giving their due to the man who sired them. Otherwise there might have been hell to pay, and no son wanted to be known for disrespecting his father. Even her sisters moved away as soon as they could, Annie got married and Breda worked as a tavern cook in the city. When their mother died, she was the one left behind to care for him.

"But you're right, the others don't exist for him," she conceded as a ribbon of parings dropped onto the paper in her lap. "It's strange, though. When the babies were born, your grandfather was right there for his turn to hold each one." She tossed the potato into the pot. "He looked them over. Not checking for ten fingers or toes like anyone might, mind you, but something..." Mary sighed and picked another potato.

"I remember," Annie offered. "I saw it too, but couldn't put a finger on it. What do you think he was looking for?"

"Something special, something only he could know." Mary looked at her daughter. Annie stopped peeling and stared at her mother expectantly, waiting for her to go on.

"It was different when Bridget was born," she continued. "I can remember that day like it was yesterday, it surprised me so." She paused as she recalled the incident. "All the other babies he held for a minute and then handed them right back to their mother. Even Jason, the first great-grandson to carry on the family name. I thought Ownie would cry when he handed him back to Kathleen." Mary stared unfocused at the opposite wall. "Bridget was different. He held her to his cheek, a faint whisper in her wee ear. He got up from his chair and looked like he dared anyone to take her away. He brought her out here to the porch and I thought Maureen would have a fit, she was so scared." Mary stopped, lost again in her memory of the day.

"Then what?" Annie verbally nudged her mother. "He didn't hurt the baby, right?"

"Good heavens, no!" Mary went back to peeling. "After about ten minutes, I got a little nervous myself and came out to see. He was sitting in this very chair with the baby still against his cheek. He never said a word, just looked at me with the oddest expression, like I interrupted something important. He held the baby out to me and I gathered her in my arms. He went directly to his room, shut the door and never came out again for the rest of the day."

Annie pondered for a minute. "But then he forgot her too, didn't he? She was as invisible as the other kids, until that day."

"Until that day," repeated Mary, again pausing while the memory played itself out in her mind. "I was scared to death. I looked high and low but I couldn't find her anywhere. I prayed to the Blessed Mother to keep her safe." She stopped and sighed. "Then I heard Ownie's voice through the door. I opened it just a crack and peeked in. She was cradled on his lap and he was telling her a story. It wasn't a tale I'd ever heard him tell before. And that's where she goes every afternoon, after her nap. He tells her the old stories. That's all."

Annie stared at her mother, potato poised in mid-air with her mouth open. "I still don't think it's right," was all she could think of to say.

* * *

The little one opened her eyes slowly and looked up into the old man's face. His knobby hand dropped back to his knee. She reached up her own plump hand and patted his cheek.

"We're almost done, right Ownie?" she asked.

"Yes, pet, we are almost done," he whispered back hoarsely and kissed her forehead.

He was tired. These lessons were necessary, but exhausted him. He knew his time was near and he had given her almost all now. She knew too. She was next in the line that stretched back to the ancient ones. He had waited a long time for her, but he knew there had to be another to take his place. The line would not be broken. He was content his burden was almost done and now she would be The Keeper. She would preserve the old stories, safeguarding them as he had, as all those before them had done. He adored this childas he had no other in his life, save one. His time with each of them had been so short, yet filled with such intense love.

"I will miss you, Ownie," she said so sadly he wanted to fold her in his arms and hold her to him forever. She climbed down from his lap and walked slowly to the door. She turned and looked, put her pudgy little hand to her mouth and blew him a kiss. Then she left, closing the door softly behind her.

He sighed and knuckled a tear that threatened to spill down his cheek. He remembered the other one, his grandmother. He knew now what she must have felt those many years ago, when he had been the one who curled into her lap. He knew, too, what the little one felt now. He didn't envy her the obligation she must carry for so many years to come, as he had lived with it himself. It had not been easy, but it had been necessary. She would be the one apart, because she was the chosen one, never because she chose for herself. He sighed deeply and closed his eyes.

Bridget stepped onto the porch. Her aunt and grandmother started, looking at her uneasily. She walked to the edge of the stairs and nudged open the door while she turned to face them.

"Ownie's almost through," she said in a voice that sounded far wiser than a four-year-old should have. Then she walked down the steps and across the lawn.

"What was that supposed to mean?" Annie asked, her mouth a puzzled frown.

"I'm not sure," Mary answered her daughter. "I'm not quite sure."

* * *

When she opened the door this day, the old man was wide awake and his blue eyes, as bright as her own, sparkled down at her. She thought he looked happy and sad at the same time. She climbed into his lap.

"This is the last story, isn't it, Ownie?"

"Yes, pet, today is the last one." He stroked her hair. "This is the story of Owen. The others I have told you as my grandmother told me, and as her father told her. I tell you now of my own days as you will speak your own tale when it is your time and the next one has come to you..."

When he finished the story, he inhaled sharply and his hand slipped from her curls. She sat patiently for a moment and watched. His eyes closed, the lids like thin crinkled paper stretched across the darkened hollows. She reached up a hand to each side of his face and gently stroked his cheeks. When she kissed his thin lips, she thought he smiled.

"I love you so much, Ownie," she whispered as she gazed at the familiar furrows of his worn face. "Have a good sleep."

Bridget climbed down and tiptoed out of the room. This time she left the door open. She walked through the kitchen, pushed open the screen door and stepped onto the porch where her aunt and grandmother were sitting. When they turned to look, her wide blue eyes glistened with tears.

"You better go see, Nana," she said to her grandmother. "Ownie's all through now."

* * *

The day of the funeral was fittingly overcast with an occasional drip of rain. The family gathered at the grave, open and waiting for the old man's casket to be lowered. Bridget looked up at her mother, Maureen, as she held her hand. They stood at the very front of the crowd gathered to pay respects, next to her grandmother Mary, waiting for the ceremony to begin.

"The angels are crying for Ownie," the little girl said as she looked up at her mother's face.

"Yes, pet, I suppose they are." Maureen's forehead creased with surprise at her daughter's comment.

"Mammy, I'm going to miss Ownie an awful lot." Bridget pouted and her eyes glistened with tears. "Do you think he'll ever come back to visit?"

Maureen gasped but composed herself before she answered. "I don't think so, pet. Ownie's gone for a good long sleep up in heaven now, with the angels."

"That's good," Bridget sighed. "He was very tired."

Maureen turned to whisper to her mother. Bridget looked at the scene around her. She saw the priest coming around the side of the tent over the grave. Everyone else must have seen him too, as their murmurings dwindled to silence. The priest made the sign of the cross and began to recite the prayers for the dead. The mourners answered by rote, responses ingrained from years of repetition.

Bridget's mind wandered. She remembered random bits of Ownie's stories. She had her favorites, but she remembered all of them, even the ones that were not so nice. She had to remember, it was what she had been chosen for. She didn't really understand why, but she knew she would when she was older. There was a very important thing she had to do today, though, of that she was certain, and it was almost time. She turned her attention back to the service. The priest waved his hands in the air above the casket.

"That's the box where Ownie's sleeping," Bridget whispered and secretly pointed.

The priest finished the prayers and the last *Amen* echoed across the cemetery. The crowd broke into smaller groups as the immediate family gathered at the side of the tent. Nobody seemed in much of a hurry. The priest stepped away to a knot of men who had known the old man in his younger days. Bridget took advantage of her mother's conversation with a cousin she hadn't seen in years to break away from her grip. Her short legs trotted over to where her grandmother was talking to her sister while they waited for the other siblings to pray over the coffin. She tilted her head and looked up at their faces. Nobody was paying attention to the little girl.

Bridget walked to the back side of the coffin, carefully avoiding the edge of the deep hole. She peeked around the side but nobody looked her way, all involved in their own business. The coffin looked huge to her, made of shiny dark wood. A wide decorative molding bordered the edge of the lid with three brass handles spaced beneath it. The little girl grabbed hold of the center handle and hoisted herself up on her toes to a narrow ledge around the bottom of the casket. She peered over the top. Nobody noticed as she climbed on top of the coffin. She carefully stood up to her full height on the rounded lid and spread her arms wide as she gazed at the sky.

"Jesus, Mary and Joseph!" Mary cried out as she spotted her granddaughter standing on top of the coffin.

"Oh my God!" Maureen yelled as she spied her daughter at the same time.

Cries and shouts went up from the crowd. Several women started to run toward the coffin but were pulled up short before they reached the tent. Mary got there first and tried to grab Bridget but was prevented from reaching the little girl. Maureen cried hysterically, rooted to the ground where she stood. Aunts and uncles and cousins gathered around the scene but no one was able to get close to Bridget. As one, they fell silent and stopped wherever they were.

A fresh breeze lifted the flaps of the tent and played with the flowers that had been placed around the grave, tossing loose petals into the air around the little girl. Frozen in place, every eye was focused on her face. Bridget's voice pealed loud and clear, with the innocent tone of a four-year-old, yet ancient in its timbre. There wasn't another sound. No one there would have seen or heard the likes of it, nor had it been heard for eighty years, since the young Owen had spoken the words in his turn.

"Eoin Mac Brigid has returned to the old ones, passing the words on to Brigid Ní Eoin. Is mise coimeádaí an scéil! I am The Keeper!"

Thunder cracked overhead. One brilliant flash engulfed the bronze curls and innocent expression, casting the child's visage with fiery gold for one instant. Another flash embraced the casket and a golden orb ascended to the sky in front of her. Her blue eyes gleamed as she watched the image of her beloved grandfather soar into the procession of his waiting ancestors. Another rumble and the light was gone, returning the day as it was.

Bridget blinked and looked out over her family gathered around her. They were her responsibility now. The stories had been entrusted to her, to protect with diligence and ruthlessness, though it would not be the challenge it was for those who had come before her long ago. In those ancient times, they defended from those who would try to seize the words, steal them for their own gain against the tribe, but that was not the case anymore. These days, most weren't even aware the stories existed. Still, she would do what was required of her, and when the time was right, she would pass the stories to the one who would come after her, another yet to be born. It was the way and as it should be. The little girl knew that Ownie would be waiting for her when her time had come. She lowered her arms, and in an instant, the spell that had been raised was released. Mary took one long step and reached out for her granddaughter, grabbing her around the waist and pulling the child against her.

"Mother Mary, what were you thinking, child?" The grand-mother was breathing as hard as if she had run a mile to get there. "Are you all right, pet?"

Maureen reached them next and threw her arms around both her mother and daughter at the same time. "What were you doing, Bridget? You're near to being the death of me."

Both women cried as they hugged the little girl as she squirmed to release their hold. All around them, the relatives pressed to know if she was all right, called her a little monkey and a bold one. The younger cousins pointed, sure that a spanking would be in order. The priest was pale as if he had seen a ghost. But there was no memory of what they had witnessed, the rite of passage from one Keeper to the next. Only Bridget knew. She broke free of her mother and grandmother and stood looking up at the sky.

"I love you, Ownie. I promise I will do good."

The Backwards Princess of Unusual Parentage

Allison Mulder

Allison Mulder writes fantasy, science fiction, and horror. Her short fiction has appeared in Fireside Fiction, Escape Pod, and more. You can find her at allisonmulder.wordpress.com, or on Twitter as @AMulderWrites.

The queen did love her magic mirror, just as the rumors claimed.

He pointed out all her mistakes. He helped her weigh political decisions, envisioning every consequence or potential benefit. Together, back-to-back with the enchanted glass barrier between them, they sorted through her throne-seeking suitors—ruling out those solely obsessed with beauty, or bogged down by bad families, or otherwise bothersome in ways that blossomed to disasters within the mirror's future-sight. And when the two of them decided no other suitor was suitable, the mirror reflected back all the queen's best qualities and shaped them into a child within her womb.

But the queen's love for her mirror was not a blind one.

She folded her hands over her stomach, flushed and giddy from the magic, yet apprehensive. "What price must I pay?"

"No price," said her mirror. "Not from me. The child is a gift, and I ask for nothing."

"A gift," the queen repeated, only more guarded. "But I wasn't asking for just your price."

In all the generations of royalty who'd occupied the Palace of the Mirror and consulted the sorcerers beyond the glass, the mirror men had never bestowed a gift without some expectation of return. They favored tricky deals and driving hard bargains, and the queen's mirror had been their spokesman since long-ago days before they crafted the mirror itself, when a stone fortress was still shelter enough for them. He was the best of the sorcerers—the guardian of the looking glass gate. He was not meant to give away magic hand over fist, channeling so much of it through his own being—more than the others had freely offered up.

"What will they ask of me?" the queen asked gently, and her mirror looked away.

"The spell required more power than I anticipated," he said. "For the highest kind of working, they'll expect the usual highest price."

"A royal's firstborn child," the queen said. Thorns sprouted in her tone, despite herself. "This was not among the possible outcomes you showed me."

"Would it have stopped you?" he asked.

No. She'd have asked for the child no matter the cost. But it complicated matters, and she moved to the other side of the bed, farthest from where the mirror hung.

She was old enough to remember the last high price. Her older brother, traded away in exchange for crops that would grow through winter, sustaining the kingdom until its famine ended. She remembered him stepping out of the mirror once every few years, at odd hours, and ordering the palace staff about—a tyrant. He'd been the firstborn prince, after all. Then he would leave the palace, and return days or weeks later with powerful relics stowed in his bag, couriering them for the mirror men as bartered firstborns had done for ages. Until, eventually, like every other courier, he'd died.

All the stories agreed: traded firstborns inevitably grew cruel, but they never grew old.

"If they'll want her, then what was this for?" the queen asked, hands forming fists.

"They'll never succeed at taking her," her mirror said. "Even if they strike me down and replace me as guardian, they can't pass through the glass—not anymore."

When the sorcerers walled up their magic behind mirrors, they'd walled up themselves with it, forsaking the world and their stone palace in favor of a stranger fortress. Though they watched through every mirror, they could not walk beyond the glass—couldn't even hear or speak into the world apart from through the lone gate.

"Hide our daughter from their sight, as best you can," the queen's mirror whispered. "Make plans beyond this room, where none of us will hear. They'll watch for her after the birth, as they watch you even now, but I promise you, they won't be able to lay a hand on her."

"Yes. Alright." The queen rubbed her temples. "I'll keep our child from all the mirrors. Her own reflection will remain a stranger to her."

The mirror had often pointed out the queen's stubbornness as a flaw, but now he thought it was among the fairest of her qualities.

"After the birth," he agreed. "For now, don't leave this mirror's sight."

"So the magic will hold?" the queen asked.

Her mirror flushed a delicate pink. "And so I can watch her forming."

The queen nodded. She moved nearer to the mirror's surface. Afterall, the child was as much his as it was hers.

* * *

The queen remained by the mirror's side for the entirety of her pregnancy. Because of that, a perfectly normal birth still suffered under persistent rumors. Everyone laughed that the child must've come out backward, and probably vain.

Everyone laughed, except the princess herself as she grew older.

"I can't be backwards!" The child's wail became familiar throughout the palace halls. "People look the same both-ways."

But she was left-handed, and her mother's exact freckles were dashed across her cheeks in reverse. She read backwards faster than forwards, even aloud, and her feet always went wrong in dancing lessons, carrying her in directions that completely opposed her teacher's instructions. Though of course—when abandoned to feel out her own footing—she could mirror his movements beautifully.

The princess also behaved a bit backwardly, always dangling upside-down from tree limbs or conversing with the lowest servants like they were her very own siblings. But these odd strokes only made everyone love the princess, even more than they loved their queen.

They teased her anyway, relentlessly, a very specific purpose to their prodding. A mandate passed along in whispers and rumors, ever since the queen gave birth and removed every mirror from the palace rooms. Plagued by the tall tales surrounding her birth, the princess quickly developed a strong aversion to mirrors.

Not all reflections could be avoided. There were the palace's reflecting pools, which the queen regretted but couldn't bear to remove—not after all her grandmother's efforts to construct them. There was the gleaming of guards' armor—many soldiers obstinately hovering at the princess's side, convinced the mirror men could be beaten back by simple blades. There was glass, there was polished marble, there was faceted jewelry on the necks of gaudy guests. Some of these things were avoidable. Most weren't.

But these only offered the mirror men glimpses of their promised princess. Fragments and flickers, enough to heighten their desire, but not enough for them to act on it.

As long as the princess stayed out of her mother's bedroom, where the magic mirror hung, all would be well.

But one day, the princess sat down to read beside a reflecting pool. A chapter into the text, she noticed thin frost settling across the still water's surface. Not in a wave so much as a bloom—a puff, like breath fogging a winter window. Just as the princess shot to her feet, letters formed, as if drawn by invisible fingers.

The words were backwards. The princess read them in an instant, before the guards idling nearby even noticed her standing.

We can show you your father.

The princess stilled. She knew the circumstances around her birth—how the queen never strayed from her magic mirror for purposes she refused to reveal—but what came before, the other half of the backwards girl's whole, was still a mystery to the princess.

As the guards rushed over—ready to attack whatever disturbed her—the words vanished. Others appeared in their place.

Come to your mother's magic mirror.

The princess tossed her head, banishing all her curiosity. She'd been warned how the mirror men liked to play tricks, especially on firstborn royals. If they'd had a hand in her more eccentric qualities—as she'd long suspected—then she'd had quite enough of them.

Much as she wondered who her father was, she didn't care enough to become gullible. And she'd already resolved to rule without the mirror's counsel—the first such monarch in many generations.

She enunciated her next words at the foggy water so clearly that anyone would know them by sight, if not by hearing: "No. Never."

The frost cloud vanished, her reflection reappearing, only—

The princess screamed, and fear rippled through the palace in the hearts of all who heard.

The queen hoisted her skirts above her knees and hurtled down hallways toward the garden, swearing under her breath. "Those damn reflecting pools—"

She was not the first to reach her daughter, but everyone cleared a path for their queen. The princess—sun-browned and perfect as ever—trembled in the arms of one flustered guard, sobbing with her face turned away from his gleaming armor.

Her reflection in the metal—and in the water, too—was of a monster. A ghoulish, fang-toothed beast, with tears dappling the collar of its dress.

* * *

The queen sat on her bedroom floor, back pressed against the subdued mirror.

"They're impatient for a child who can pass through the mirror unharmed," he said, words scarcely audible through the thick, black curtain his queen had hung across the glass. "So much of their magic expended, with no return...but I didn't know they would spend more power casting illusions like that. They don't trust me anymore."

"I should send her away," the queen said, lips trembling.

Her mirror spoke hollowly. "Please don't."

They sat in silence, though words and music had always been the best things between them—the only things they had to themselves. They always felt eyes watching, but that night the mirror men's combined gaze held a sharper edge, the sensation cutting every line of conversation short.

"Is she beautiful?" the mirror asked finally. "As beautiful as you?"

The queen scoffed. Then pressed her palm flat against the glass. It warmed under his touch on the other side. For a few moments, their skin met. Lingered. Then the world beyond the looking glass pained the queen's lover, and he drew his hand back, hissing in pain through his teeth.

"You could look at her through the reflections," the queen said slowly. "The way all the other mirror men do."

"No," her mirror said. "I'm afraid to see her. Afraid I'd let them bring her here, just as they desire."

The queen wanted to protest, but both of them knew the truth:

he'd gone with the other thousand sorcerers when they chose to hoard their power in a place beyond anyone's reach. He'd been the thousand and first of them—the one who sat down at the doorway and promised to keep out any thieves, conquerors, or desperate beggars seeking spells.

"I should smash you," the queen said, her voice breaking.

The mirror said nothing at first. Then, timorously, "I'm not sure you could, my love."

She sprang to her feet and kicked the mirror's center with her full weight focused through her heel.

The glass did not shatter.

She beat at the mirror until she was breathless, until she was sobbing, until she somehow stumbled into sleep, curled at the mirror's base. The mirror whispered soft and pretty things, and played the pipes she'd always loved to listen to.

The glass remained whole.

And the thousand pairs of eyes watched on.

* * *

Everyone told the princess half-truths.

The monsters constantly looming in her reflections were a trick played by the mirror men, who were cross at her mother, the queen. A deal gone wrong—sour politics the princess didn't have to concern herself with until she was older.

For her part, the princess said nothing of the mirror men's offer to reveal her father's identity. She remembered long-ago talk of sending her away—whispers of towers with nothing that gleamed or shone—and she didn't want to leave her mother's side, or her home.

In consequence, the princess's aversion to mirrors turned to loathing. And the mirror she hated most was the one in the queen's bedroom, which led to the mirror men's stronghold.

Everyone took some solace in that, knowing the backwards girl wouldn't stumble onto her own doom as a result of simple curiosity.

But the queen remained uneasy, knowing her daughter might reverse her position if she ever learned the whole truth of the deal that brought her into being. If she ever learned just how much of the queen's mirror went into making the backwards princess.

He was the best of the mirror men, the guardian between worlds, and the greatest traitor to those who lived on the other side of the looking glass. By the loosest definitions in either world, he was most certainly the princess's father.

And the queen knew the lure of realizing family lay beyond the mirror's surface. She remembered creeping down hallways at midnight, desperate for a glimpse of the brother traded for the kingdom's wellbeing, even after she'd learned of his vicious nature.

So all through the princess's childhood, the queen held her silence. She swore her servants to secrecy. She warped the truth as needed, seeding a dozen new rumors through the kingdom to grow over the singular truth.

The princess collected all these seeds, turning various theories round and round in her head, determined to figure out her parentage without the help of any crooked, scheming sorcerers. It wasn't a mystery she considered every day. But it was the question she returned to in quiet moments, on occasional sleepless nights, or during the hours she spent memorizing the lineage of her family. There was a rhythm to the string of names and stations, and the absence before the princess's own name felt glaring and wrong in her mouth. As wrong as the somewhat truncated details of former firstborns sent beyond the mirror.

One day in the garden—far from the reflecting pools—the princess saw two servants walking, the older instructing the younger. Their heads held the tilt of gossipers, and the senior maid had become a loud talker since her hearing began to go.

The princess didn't often witness the arrival and instruction of new servants. By the time she met them, they'd always been made quieter and more careful than they might've otherwise been—the same way the princess received meals with every sharp bone plucked out, or wooden playthings with all the splinters sanded off.

The princess sprinted across a flowerbed and through a line of tall, shaped shrubs in order to get ahead of the pair, and then she climbed the tall, shady tree where people always lingered on the path.

It was a hot day, and the two gossipers lingered a long time. The princess listened through half an hour of serving etiquette, the proper way to fold sheets, and how best to address a princess who constantly ignored rules of decorum.

Then, finally, she overheard an innocent slip.

"And don't ask after the princess's sire," the senior maid said, hand cupped around her too-loud murmur.

"Is it something very scandalous?" the younger asked, a softer whisper.

The princess strained her ears, willing the tree's leaves to stop rustling, willing her tiring fingers to hold firm just a little longer.

The senior maid raised her shoulders, hands spread in bemusement. "Well we all know it's the mirror itself, but no one's very sure how it was done, and anyway, it's an impolite topic."

White rage knifed through the princess.

How it was done.

She could guess how the monsters in the mirror had done it. Tricks and traps and hurting—

Her grip slipped from the smooth-barked branches, and she landed in a crumpled heap at the servants' feet.

"Princess!" The servants fussed over her, the scratches on her palms, the bloody bump on the back of her head, but the backwards girl waved them off.

"I want to see my mother," she said, shaking.

"Of course you do." The newer of the servants took the girl by the hand, rushing her down hallways as the senior maid went to find her majesty.

The princess shook her hand free as she entered the queen's extravagant rooms, and spoke coldly. "You're dismissed."

"I don't think—"

She rounded on the young maid, as if it was something she did all the time. "Your princess is dismissing you."

The maid flinched. She glanced at the curtain separating the queen's parlor from her bedroom. She must have already been told, as all the servants were, that the princess was not to be left alone in her mother's room.

The princess grimaced. "I'm sorry. My head hurts. Fetch a healer while I wait for Mother?"

"Of course." The maid flinched again. "My lady."

She left.

The backwards princess straightened her skirts. She searched the room for a weapon by the light of the windows overlooking the gardens, and settled on a small, heavy statuette of polished black stone.

She whipped back the curtain like she'd done it a hundred times. And she stepped into the queen's bedroom.

The mirror was still half-draped in black curtains, but the sound of pipes drifted from one exposed corner—a song the princess had heard her mother humming.

It stopped suddenly as the princess's shoe tapped on the tile floor.

"Dear?" the queen's mirror asked. Uncertain. Because it didn't sound like the queen's footfalls, but who else would approach the mirror she always cleaned with her own regal hands?

That word, Dear, stopped the princess. It did not sound like a snare, or some kind of noose binding her mother's neck.

She took hold of the curtain just as the queen and the senior maid arrived at the parlor door.

She threw off the black fabric just as the queen cried out.

The backwards princess and the queen's mirror stared at each other, still as portraits, each of them seeing the similarities, the differences, the links reversed and traversed between them.

The princess dropped the stone statue, breathing hard enough to fog the glass.

"Hello, Father," she said.

Two thousand eyes of a thousand mirror men fixed on the girl they'd been promised, and they all surged forward, fingers passing through the glass and brushing the princess's wrist.

The queen ran forward, arms outstretched.

And the queen's mirror—the princess's father by anyone's definition—balled up his fist and slammed it knuckles-first into the other side of the glass, cracking it into a thousand and one falling shards.

A Recipe for Trouble

Aimee Ogden

Aimee Ogden is a former science teacher and software tester; now she writes about sad astronauts and angry princesses. Her novellas "Sun-Daughters, Sea-Daughters" and "Local Star" debuted in 2021 from Tor.com and Interstellar Flight Press respectively.

Leah has always felt compelled to touch every book at the sale, to inspect every cover, searching for that one special discovery. Her mother doesn't mind; she knows all the adults here and she stops to talk to each of them. So when Leah finds WORLD OF DESSERTS, its cover sticky and its pages smelling faintly of smoke, at the bottom of a pile of history books, she cracks it open to see what's inside.

Cramped handwriting fights for space in the margins of the pages. Leah's mouth crimps: she loves to find old math and Spanish and literature textbooks, hates to find their questions already marked with answers by someone else's pen. But then she realizes what the words *say*, what they *are*, and she snaps the book closed with a dangerous thrill.

The book goes into Mom's basket under a few decoys: two Harry Potter novels, *Computer Science for Dummies* , and some cheap dime-store novel with an underdressed sorceress on the front. Mom prunes these from the pile without interrupting her conversation with two of the ladies from church. Harry Potter books and sorcery and half-nude ladies all fall under the broad heading of *satanism*.

Or maybe the watchword these days is *worldliness*; that would catch the programming book, too. Leah hoped that one would slide past; she's unsurprised that it fails. She and her mother have already gone several rounds about whether a tenth-grade young lady belongs in Advanced Programming, among a bunch of slavering junior and senior boys.

In any case, she doesn't even think to check a cookbook for an infestation of occultism.

Leah bides over three snappish, irritable days of algebra and Catechism homework, laundry-folding, toilet-scrubbing. The secret of the cookbook pulses raw and electric at the back of her mouth, painful as a broken tooth. When she can bear no more of the tender suspense, she shuts her door and sits with her back to it, pawing through pages, fingers lingering over antique stains.

She chooses more quickly than she wants to. A closed door, in this house, is more of an invitation than an open one.

* * *

DEEP DISH BROWNIES and Incantation for Impenetrable Good Mood

- 8 Tbsp butter (plus more for pan) Soften using body heat while you meditate on peacefulness list the factors outside your control

- ¾ cup white sugar

½ cup white flour

½ cup cocoa powder

- Pinch of salt * Another pinch of salt (throw over shoulder of dominant hand when taking brownies out of oven)

- ½ tsp baking powder
- 2 eggs
- 12 oz dark chocolate, finely chopped choc chips OK too ...

* * *

Leah's glasses fog over when she opens the oven. At the aroma alone, she dissolves into giggles, although that may just be nerves. Before it cools, she heaves a wet, crumbling slice onto a plate and breathes chocolatey dragon-steam around the first bite.

She's still leaning against the counter, chasing crumbs around the plate with a saliva-slick fingertip, when her mother enters the kitchen. Leah stands still while her mother moves around her to pull out garlic salt and basil and the good knife and the cutting board and the frying pan, fencing Leah in with sharp quiet little comments about spoiled appetites and spilled crumbs.

The words pierce her, as they always do. But this time, nothing comes pouring out through the open wounds. Her smile does not dry out, her pulse does not skip and hammer in her throat. She cuts herself another slice and eats it, sucking melted chocolate off her fingers, while her mother pretends not to hear. The magic is real, whether it comes from some secret and unknowable aether or from the biochemical thrill of rebellion and motivational salience.

* * *

PARTY PUNCH for a Rainy Day
- 2 liter bottle lemon-lime soda (Sprite most reliable, mixed results with 7-Up/ Fresca/off-brand)

**UNDER NO CIRCUMSTANCES USE MOUNTAIN DEW

• 1 tub orange sherbet slightly softened under a tepid shower

• Fresh strawberry slices Mash strawberries while reciting the 7-day weather forecast

* * *

On the laundry line, sheets snap and strain against their pins. One tears loose at the far corner, flapping ominously like a lumberjack's plaid-printed ghost. Leah's mother yanks it down and shoves it into the basket just as the first drops strike, pebbling the still-hanging laundry with fat round circles. Leah's brothers just barely beat her inside; they ditch their bikes in the middle of the yard while she runs lopsided, the basket balanced on one hip.

Leah is waiting just inside the kitchen door beside her neatly stacked piles of the last laundry load: just-so squares of washcloth, balled-up socks, a rainbow of underwear. She passes sweating plastic cups into hands as her soaked family stumbles into the shelter of the house.

Her mother's laden basket drops to the linoleum floor, vomiting wet pillowcases and souvenir t-shirts from places they've never been. She thanks Leah, sincerity sewn tight with bafflement. Leah has never been much help in the kitchen; indeed, she has yet to live down the fire-alarm infamy of the blackened grilled cheese she made last fall.

Over the rim of her plastic cup, Leah looks for the hidden tell of suspicion in her mother's face: a sideways glance as she marks down some furtive sin and treasures it up against a future need, a tightness in the skin around her eyes as she seeks to see through Leah's virtuous façade. Leah finds nothing, which she hopes means her mother does, too.

* * *

Chocolate Silence Souffle

- 2 marshmallows (hold in each cheek while baking. Eat when finished?)
- ¼ cup sugar
- 1 cup finely diced dark chocolate (unsweetened baking chocolate = best effect, don't go less than 85%)
- 1.5 tsp vanilla extract
- 4 egg yolks + 4 egg whites First remove the contents of a single egg by blowing. Whisper your heaviest secret into the hollow shell before disposal ...

* * *

How can Leah weigh a secret? How can she choose a single one, when they all writhe and slip so tightly together, greasy and labyrinthine, unpleasant to linger on and impossible to separate?

She puts the wet, slippery eggshell to her lips. When she exhales, her cool breath finds her fingertip at the hole on the far side. She closes her eyes. She tells the egg what her mother already knows—that she is a bad person, a lust-soaked neoplasm, tumescent with wrath and pride and a million other smaller, duller sins too petty to name—and what her mother does not—that she *does not want to be better.*

The house is quiet: the boys half-heartedly kicking a soccer ball in the backyard, her mother sweeping out the garage or weeding the garden. Cleaning, always cleaning, her only real hobby. It's not fair for Leah to hate that about her, but she does anyway.

Leah locks the door of her room and puts her back against it. She eats the entire soufflé until her stomach aches pleasantly and the background sounds of the house have bled away. No thrumming washing machine, no droning attic fan.

She hates herself a little, for finding real magic and putting it to such venal purposes. Still, she hikes down her too-tight shorts and slides her hand inside her underwear. No one but her can hear the hitch of her breath and the soft thick pounding of her palm against her own skin. When she's done, sweat-sticky and halfway to bruised, she hates herself a little for that, too.

* * *

Single Crust Open-Mind Peach Pie
- Half recipe for double pie crust (p. 97)
- 5-7 fresh peaches, ripe Bury each pit in the garden along with one painful memory
- ¾ cup white sugar + 1 pinch - slip into the shoes of the person to be persuaded
- 1 tbsp butter + 1 dab to grease the plate of the person to be persuaded
- 1/3 cup white flour

- ½ tsp cinnamon
- ~~¼ nutmeg~~ no one likes nutmeg, use a dash of allspice or cloves ...

* * *

The kitchen smells of burnt cloves and smoke. The little glass jar has fallen open between the burners of the stovetop, brown-black powder discoloring the white enamel range and smoking where it touches the hot burner. Flecks of ash spin through the air and settle gently onto the spilled spices.

Leah stands in the corner, arms folded tight against herself, as her mother tears page after page from the cookbook and scorches them out of existence. Fragments of the paper waft past on the heat-addled air currents, blocky black text and soft loops of half-familiar handwriting. Fragments of speech, too, her mother unable to assemble a coherent thought or a grammatical sentence. *Witchcraft—something evil invited into this house—so careless—disobedient.*

Leah doesn't cry and she doesn't argue. She *is* disobedient; disobedient and sarcastic and impatient and full of lies. A shopping list of ingredients for a truly vile human casserole. There's nothing her mother can say to her that she hasn't already said to herself. The only real difference is that her mother has the power to punish her with something more substantial than self-recrimination.

The cookbook's empty covers fall to the counter like the skin sloughed off by a creature growing into something bigger and stranger. Something too much to be contained any longer. Leah's mother wipes her soot-streaked hands on her jeans and says in a broken voice that she needs to go call the pastor.

Leah stays behind. An orange-edged scrap of paper loops in front of her. It requests her *eaviest secre* before the glowing embers chew away the letters and leave only darkness behind.

* * *

After that, Leah plays the part. The rage that boils inside of her does not escape in tea-kettle shrieks; disdain sparks but, in the airless hollow of her chest, its fire is not permitted to catch. She obeys before she is tasked, answers mildly when questioned, accepts punishments—*"consequences"*—whether or not she has earned them.

Normalness settles back over the house, smothering whatever flames of disgust and disappointment still lick at her mother. Normalness is her mother's golden calf; above all else she desires to feel normal, to appear normal to the outside eyes she feels constantly peering in through the windows of the world all round.

Leah is in ninth grade. She knows very well how to feign *normal*.

She broaches the subject of her fall class schedule over dinner one night. She sits on her hands, to warm them as well as to keep herself from picking at the chipped chicken on toast, and speaks in a tumble. To give her words weight, she hides her ugliest secrets, all the hymns she doesn't mean and all the books she's not supposed to read and all the words she's said and can never take back, so that what she says comes out heavy. Sorrowful. *Convincing.*

Instead of telling her mother what she wants—a guarantee of disappointment—she asks: can she please (a hand-crafted please, artisanal, the load-bearing structure of the sentence) sign up for computer programming, if she takes home ec as well?

Her arguments are martialed and waiting in reserve, an attractive story of preparing for my future and being able to help you more around the house. Her private motives stay safely stitched up inside: the knowledge and opportunity to recreate a magical soufflé—perhaps even to create a recipe new and wonderful with magic all her own.

Her mother sets down her fork with a careful smile. Leah will take home economics, she decrees, with punitive precision; she has failed to demonstrate the grace that might have earned her enrollment in computer science.

Leah accepts the sacrifice of her decoy with dignity and a rich, decadent joy.

Gentle Ways to Kill a Dragon

Kit Harding

Kit Harding is a writer and librarian who belongs to the cities and wilds of New England. Her work has previously appeared in the Zombies Need Brains anthology Derelict, and she cohosts the Magic podcast WNXS News on MTG Nexus. You can find her online at https://writerkit.dreamwidth.org

"There are some people who might suggest that trying to take on a dragon by yourself is not a great idea, you know. There are some people who might suggest that wandering up a mountain without telling anyone where you're going is a foolish choice. But you're so convinced you can't ask anyone for help and it never once occurs to you that your perceptual issues mean you are not exactly well-placed to judge whether trying a suicidal stunt is a good idea."

The steady stream of Gregor's complaints were the first thing that penetrated the darkness surrounding me. For a moment I didn't move at all, just letting his words wash over me, but then memory came crashing down on me and I snapped open my eyes and sat up. Or tried to, anyway; pain in my side stopped me and I let out a soft shriek. Gregor was immediately beside me.

"Don't try to move," he said. "Don't sit up. You will stay here until the storm subsides." A thunderclap sounded outside, punctuating this sentence. "At a minimum. If you aren't well enough to move by then you will stay here longer than until the storm subsides."

I subsided back onto what was apparently a bedroll laid atop a small stone slab. Looking around, I was in some sort of mountain cave. There was a small fire burning near the cave mouth. Outside, a storm raged.

"Why am I here?" I demanded.

"Why are you here, in this cave? Or why are you alive?"

"You know the answer to that."

"I suspect the answer to that," he said. "I don't know the answer to that until you say it."

"Despite your rant earlier, you know I'm not the kind of person who goes off for needless heroics."

"And yet, I found you on the mountain with a dragon almost on top of you, and no evidence that you'd tried to run even though I know you're more than capable of getting away once you realized you couldn't kill it on your own."

"Who says I was trying to kill it on my own?"

"Well if you weren't, then either you have terrible allies or you've now learned that dragons aren't amenable to talking." Gregor's tone was acidic, leaving me no doubt he knew which of those things it was. He always labeled these things as 'guesses' and insisted he didn't know what was in my head until I told him, but his so-called guesses were right nearly all of the time.

I rolled my eyes. "None of the above," I said.

"So what were you doing up there, then?"

"Killing a dragon."

"So the answer to my question is...?"

I looked away and didn't answer.

Gregor waited. He was good at waiting patiently until I said whatever I was avoiding. I was intellectually aware that dodging his question was pointless, but I still didn't actually want to come right out and say why I had been on that mountain. I was certain he'd disapprove.

"Why are you here?" I asked instead.

"You were missing, the storm was starting, and the last anyone had seen of you was going up-mountain. Right after you screamed and ran away from that dragon hunter fellow in the middle of the town square. You can see why I might be concerned about this."

"Concerned, yes, but you don't usually decide that your concern merits stalking me up-mountain."

"You don't usually decide that merely seeing someone in the square merits going up-mountain when a storm's coming and you know there's a dragon up there. Moonhunter above us, Ella, what were you thinking?"

"You never call me by name unless you're upset." It was a pitiful attempt at distraction.

"I'm not upset. And don't change the subject."

Gregor had this idea that getting upset about my well-being would somehow upset me. I had never understood why he thought that. I wouldn't have minded if he did occasionally display some emotions about me; he was so generally stoic that it was often hard to tell he cared—though he never denied having emotions. Now, I watched him begin to pace the cave agitatedly, seemingly unable to sit still, before settling back down on a rock beside the fire. Even seated, he seemed as though he might jump up again at any moment.

"When have I ever answered your questions on the first try?" I asked. "If I started giving you straight answers you'd get bored."

"I assure you, I wouldn't."

But I couldn't possibly give him a straight answer, not about this. How could I even begin to put it into words? The way the dragon hunter had looked over my body. The way he'd suggested, leeringly, that he often took the comeliest woman in the village for his reward. The way my skin had crawled even as part of me had shouted in my head *He thinks you're comely? Take a compliment!*

The way the whole village had looked the other way when he reached for me, because who could possibly gainsay the one who was going to save us all from the dragon? The way I had been dazzled at first, until I wasn't anymore?

Can't call it being forced when you were doing your duty by the village, whether you have nightmares about it afterwards or not. Can't call it being forced when you acquiesced because you'd never be allowed to refuse. But I didn't want that taint touching Gregor.

There was a problem here, though: if Gregor insisted on taking me back down the mountain, I would be helpless with these injuries for a long time. And no one would think twice about the dragon hunter visiting me when he'd already showed such signs of interest in me.

"Ella." Gregor's gentle voice broke into my thoughts and I realized I'd said nothing for such a long time I'd outlasted even his formidable patience. "Whatever it is, you can tell me about it. Whatever it is, you can talk to me. Why were you up on the mountain? Why didn't you try to get away from the dragon?"

"I was going to kill it," I said. "The dragon hunter talks and talks about going out to kill the dragon and he may have the whole village convinced he's going to do that, but he's not actually going up the mountain and doing it. Sure, eventually they'll stop believing him, but how long is that going to take and how many more people and livestock are going to die in the meantime?"

"Very good. You almost have me convinced. But if that were the whole story, you'd still have run when it became obvious you weren't fighting it off."

Once again I didn't answer. There was no answer I could make to that; not without revealing myself. He studied me for several long moments, then went to the fire at the cave mouth. In the coals was a small teapot I hadn't noticed, which he had apparently been using to heat water. Now he carefully removed it and mixed tea in the small mug he always carried with him. From the smell, it was willow bark tea, a painkiller. After a few moments to steep, he handed me the mug.

"Drink that," he said.

I briefly considered doing so, but had I wished to kill myself through toxic drug interactions I could have done that at any time, and at any rate I didn't think Gregor would be able to live with himself afterwards if he'd been the one to supply my suicide method—he would look back on it and say he should have known. So I set the mug down on the rock beside me.

"Ella, evading my questions is one thing, but you actually do need it. For the painkiller and probably also the hydration."

"If you're concerned about my hydration give me some water, then."

"It's not like you to refuse painkillers, especially when you have such obviously painful injuries."

"And yet, here I am doing exactly that. If you want to hydrate me, give me some plain water."

I watched his face carefully, because he was attentive to small details, and so I could see the moment when he figured it out. His expression was ever so briefly one of near panic before he once again hid all outward expressions of his emotion and looked at me levelly.

"What else did you take?" he asked.

I looked away.

"Ella. This is not a game. What else did you take?"

"Dragonsbane," I said. Harmless enough to me, although combined with willow bark it would have been fatal.

But saying that was enough to let him figure out the rest of it. I resolutely continued to not look at him, as I did not want to see the flash of horrified comprehension on his face. Oh, he'd hide it quickly enough and focus on projecting calm at me, but I didn't want to see it.

"Dragonsbane," he repeated, in a flat tone. "You took enough dragonsbane that you're concerned about the toxicity reaction to even this small amount of willow bark."

"Yes," I said.

"You were never planning on coming down the mountain alive at all, were you?"

"One life against the whole village," I said. "Dragon eats me, dragon dies, that's the end of it, dragon hunter moves on deprived of his glory."

"Conveniently leaving out that you also die with that plan!"

"Is that so very important?" I snapped. "I'm just the worthless one. Just the extra one. The foolish one. The one who is so strange and fey that she's not properly honored when the dragon hunter takes an interest in her! The one who might dare gainsay him and cause him to leave without killing the thing, when no one's noticed he hasn't killed the thing yet! Half-wild! Worthless! Should have been the one taken by the dragon, not her pretty sister, who'd have enough sense to go along and feel honored for it and might bring value to her house! So yes, this plan doesn't leave me alive. I don't think that matters!"

Ever so slowly, Gregor came to kneel by my side, and took my hand in both of his. "Ella, did the dragon hunter force you?"

"Is it still force when you say yes because you know you're not going to be allowed to say no?"

"Yes."

"Is it, though? I didn't fight back. I didn't even refuse, not properly. I was reluctant, and he said it was lovely that I was so modest but that no one was going to mind as it was him, and all I could think was that if I refused more forcefully and he made an issue of it people were going to blame me for the dragon."

"Ella. That's still rape."

"You say that, but I know what they'd say, and even if anyone admitted it, he's still the dragon hunter. You've seen how everyone is—and still without even proof of what he can do."

"It wouldn't be right, it wouldn't be okay, even if we did have proof he can kill the dragon." Gregor's tone was so fierce that I was set back by it. He doesn't show emotion. He doesn't show emotion to such a degree that I have trouble conceiving of the idea that I can actually matter to him, not when he's more demonstrative with his dogs than he is with me. Except, apparently, for such brief moments as this one. For him to be showing even that little bit of feeling, the strength of his reaction must have been overpowering.

"I suspect the village would disagree," I said.

"Then they're wrong." He shifted on the rock so that he could lift my head into his lap. I smiled and nestled into the comfort. "Ella. They're wrong. And this isn't the answer."

"How can it not be?" I asked bitterly. "I die, he goes from the village, everyone gets to whisper behind their hands, and I don't have to see him leering every time I close my eyes. I don't have to go through the world feeling like I can't reach it anymore. My magic's gone from me, did you know that? Ever since that night, I can't feel the earth anymore. Can't feel the power. He took that from me. Some kind of taint, it has to be."

"The Earth-mother isn't the kind to find you broken for something that was beyond your control."

"Then why can't I feel the magic?" I poured every ounce of anguish into my tone, every moment of the panic I had felt since I left the dragon hunter's bed and first realized that I couldn't feel the magic, that I couldn't reach my center, couldn't continue with my duty—could not be a healer. "Why is my power gone? I'm supposed to be a healer. I'm supposed to have power."

"I don't know," he said. "But could the fact that you've been bottling this up inside be part of it? You've had trouble reaching the magic when you're upset before."

"I grew out of that."

"You've never been this upset. You're training to be a healer. What are the effects of trauma?"

"We haven't studied that in detail yet."

"You've had an overview. Tell me the high-level version. What are the effects of trauma?"

"Flashbacks. Emotional numbness. Uncontrollable emotions. Need for control. Often self-injury."

"Any of that sounding familiar?"

I reached up and squeezed his hand, but remained silent. It was, in fact, sounding familiar. It sounded like a lot of what I had been experiencing over the last several days. The days had been a fog where I could not truly connect with anything, but had simply gone about my rote tasks as if nothing had happened. We were learning herbalism at the moment, without any magic to it, so while we were supposed to be connecting with our magic regularly, there was nothing in class to force me to reach for it, and I had been too dazed to do anything except what I absolutely had to—though years as the outcast wild child in our village had taught me to keep up a front through any kind of emotional storm if I needed to. I had finally come back to myself enough for it to occur to me that the magic might help, that meditation and reaching for the earth was supposed to be able to help us regulate our emotions, only to find that I couldn't reach the magic. The loss of that certainty—for if there had been one thing in my life true up to that point it was that the natural world would always be there for me no matter what other humans thought of me or did to me—had been the thing that led me to come up with this plan.

If I was going to be useless, it was best for my death to mean something.

The thing was, even with Gregor here going over this, I wasn't sure there was anything wrong with my reasoning. Even if it was possible for me to reach the magic again, healers were supposed to be bastions of stability, and I didn't think I could ever be that. Without a way to earn a living... well, times were hard everywhere, and there was no good way out of that. A quick death seemed better than a slow one.

Something of my thoughts must have shown on my face, because Gregor said softly, "Talk to me, Ella."

"There's still no way out. He took my life, ruined my prospects, I can't do anything, the future's a mess... I don't want to die meaninglessly."

"So you came out here to die meaningfully instead?"

"Something like that."

He squeezed my hand again, then. "There are other ways."

"What other ways? How am I supposed to do anything? If you're right, if I am suffering from trauma or shock or whatever you want to call it, how is there any sort of answer out there for me? How is there an escape? I can't keep going, you can't look after me..."

"But none of that has happened yet. It might never happen. Wait until it does, before you decide that's the end of everything."

"So I'm just supposed to sit here waiting for something to happen? Try to go about my day knowing that it's hanging over my head?"

"It's better than deciding everything's over before anything at all has happened."

"It's not that simple," I snapped, starting to cry.

"Of course not." Gregor's voice was gentle. "You have to keep choosing it every day. Just get through today. Tomorrow will come tomorrow."

"Today there's still a dragon attacking the village," I said. "We still have to deal with that today. Or more people than just me are going to get injured by it."

"So let's make a plan for fighting it together. One that doesn't end with anyone dying. If this whole 'feed something a lot of dragons- bane and feed to the dragon' plan works as a concept, why has no one tried doing it with livestock?"

"Because then they'd have to give up livestock. If you wait for it to attack, you can hope maybe your cattle will be untouched. There's not enough dragonsbane growing to dose everybody."

Gregor winced. "So they wait for it to attack instead and hope a human dies killing it? There is something very wrong with the way most people apparently approach the world."

"That's been true for ages; you just notice it less because people actually like you."

"Moonhunter only knows why. So all we have to do is steal some- one's sheep, feed it some of that dragonsbane, bring it up here to be a target, and then pretend the dragon got it?"

"...That is not the plan I'd have gone with, but it would work. Theoretically."

"Your plan is bad," he told me. "My plan is better. Besides, that dragon hunter deserves a lot worse than us stealing the sheep intended to feast him."

I snorted. "Okay. Fine. Tomorrow, after I've recovered, we can try it your way. Do not think this constitutes any kind of promise that I will stay alive."

"I don't want you to make a promise you might not keep. I just want you to not shut me out. Now, will you please try to rest? We've got a plan. You're still injured. We're trapped up in this cave at least until the storm stops, which probably means until morning, so there's nothing we can do about it now."

"If you insist." I closed my eyes, still holding close to Gregor's hand, and considered. The world was hard, and awful, and I didn't for a second believe that killing a dragon was going to make it less hard or awful. But I could at least manage staying alive long enough to kill the dragon; Gregor would need my help figuring out dragonsbane dosing for the sheep. After that... well, anything could happen, I supposed.

Even a world that managed to be tolerable for a few more days, and maybe a few more days after that.

It was, at least, a possibility.

Skipping Back

Jeannine Clarke

Jeannine Clarke is a writer, performer, and director living in the Pacific Northwest. Her improv and directing work have been featured at Emerald City Comi-Con, Geek Girl Con, The Seattle Festival of Improv Theatre, Improvaganza in Honolulu, Hawai'i, and The Denver Improv Festival.

I'd say it started innocently enough but our parties were rarely innocent, even around Christmas time. We tried to keep it small but...well, you know how it is. In truth, I liked the big parties, and I was known for my party throwing ability. Which is to say I knew which caterers to call, and how many cases of wine to order. Having people over made our 5,000 square foot house seem homey. Of course, that night I would regret having so many people over that I didn't really know.

Susan, the only person I would have really called a close friend at this thing, showed me photos of her baby girl. We had met years ago, when she was working as a makeup artist on a film I was in. I realized I had left Susan's baby gift in my bedroom, so I excused myself and ran upstairs...and opened the door on my husband with his 25-year-old co-star.

He made some noise to start to explain or apologize. I'm not sure which because I left the room and...I skipped back. It wasn't even a decision. One moment I was seeing him there, the next my mind was turning back. How far back did I want to go? Five minutes? Twenty? Twenty. I don't exactly see time in reverse, per se. It's not like rewinding a DVD, or God, even a VHS. It is more like seeing moments through a rainy window at night.

Everything was blurred, but you have context for what those blurs mean.

Suddenly I was back downstairs, standing in front of Susan. She was talking about her baby, so she didn't notice my eyes glazing over the moment my mind snaped back into my past body. There's nothing I can do about that moment—lord knows I've tried. I'm stuck looking like an idiot with a blank expression on my face every time I skip back. Susan and I repeated nearly the same conversation we had before. But instead of going upstairs to get her present, I introduced her to a colleague. Soon after, Susan made her exit from the party and I went into the dining room to get myself a large glass of wine.

A few minutes later my husband descended the staircase, coked out of his mind. His co-star emerged five minutes later. They obviously thought they got away with their rendezvous without anyone being the wiser. I poured another glass of wine. I smiled and I laughed; inside I wanted to scream.

My husband—to protect all parties involved, let's call him "Steve"—was a not a bad man. He was smart and successful; funny and insecure. He was a hard-bodied movie star, which means in those times of "my husband and I each get three celebrities we're allowed to have sex with" he was often in people's list of three. I mean to be honest, so was I. I was turning forty in February, but I did alright. In our three years of being together, and two years of marriage, I had accepted that many people wanted to have sex with my husband. There's something about celebrity that makes normal human beings act absolutely batshit crazy. People threw themselves at him, as they did at me. My smart, funny, insecure husband was generally good about turning down the constant—and I do mean constant—flow of people throwing themselves, their nude photos, their panties, in his direction. This was the second time I had caught him coked out with some girl since we'd been married. The first time I caught him having sex with a production assistant in a bathroom at a wrap party, and I skipped back to intercept him from meeting the girl. So that sex hadn't actually happened in this timeline. Of course, even though the sex didn't happen I still remembered it happening. I started on SSRIs after that.

Steve didn't cheat unless he'd done coke, and he didn't do coke unless he was at a party and some shit brought it. The last two years of our marriage had been an obstacle course, with me trying to separate Steve from the coke and from the girls that would find him when he was on coke.

I held my glass of red wine on my patio and looked out over LA. We had a hell of a view; we ought to for the 10 million I paid for the house. At that moment I would have given anything for a Christmas with snow. LA Christmases never really seemed like Christmas to me, probably because I grew up in Cañon City, Colorado. There was a week left until Christmas, so maybe, through some miracle, a snowstorm would materialize.

The party went on another couple of hours. People slowly made their goodbyes and luckily there was no more adultery—at least, not in my marriage. Steve fell asleep on a couch as soon as I had ushered the last of our guests out the door. Not willing to go into our bedroom, I slept in the guest room instead.

The next morning a driver picked me up to go to the studio. I had just started voice work for an animated kids' movie. It was a good cast—Ian McKellen was playing a rabbit in it. I love Ian McKellen. I mean, honestly, who doesn't love Ian McKellen? I was quiet in the car, preoccupied with what had happened in my bedroom the night before.

I wondered dully why I hadn't just skipped back the night before and kept them from going upstairs? I still could; it had only been a day. The only conclusion I came to as the car pulled up to the studio was this: because I was tired. Something I had learned from skipping was that there was only so much that I could control. But those bits that I couldn't control, they came for me time and again. They were still real to me, those things I saw that didn't happen. Like ghosts I carried with me.

The longest I had gone without skipping back was two months. Most of the time when I skipped, I was just turning back minutes. Sometimes a few hours. In rare cases, a day or two. One time while on LSD, I accidently skipped back a month. It was terrifying. I had wrapped a movie and found myself reshooting the whole thing over again. I got nominated for an Oscar, which led to my new acting process—to shoot and then skip back, and do it better the second, third, or fourth time. I had been cheating at acting since I was eighteen, when I started rewinding time on any bad auditions I had. It didn't mean I always got the job, not at all. But it helped me carve out a career, and to keep me out of harm's way of the perverts and predators in Hollywood. Staying in "filming shape" at nearly forty was a breeze. I could eat anything I wanted, and just skip back to before I ate it. I had an eating disorder on a whole other level. I was a lucky girl, and I lived a charmed life. At least, that's what I believed most days. Or rather, it's what I told myself.

I wrapped my day of recording and headed home. My agent called when I got in the car and said she wanted to talk about "my next phase." I could hear what she wasn't saying, which is that I was turning forty soon and that tends to be a problem for actresses. It had started a year or two ago—I started getting the "wife" and "mom" scripts. Except that I was no good at the mom scripts because I had never been a mom. My career was cooling off and Hollywood didn't know what to do with me. *I* didn't know what to do with me. Steve was three years older than me and was being courted to play the next Bond villain. And I was voicing a deer in a kids' movie. "With Ian McKellen!" my brain snapped in reply, like a manic recording. Yes. With Ian McKellen. My career was fine. My marriage was fine except that my husband did coke and banged girls who were born after the Challenger explosion. I was in a movie with Ian McKellen. I mean, not in the same room as him. I was adjacent, tangentially associated, with Ian McKellen. It was probably better that way. If he were a jerk, I'd never know; I could continue to admire him from afar and not be disappointed. There I was, in a movie I didn't want to be in, with Ian McKellen. Everyone should be so lucky.

Steve was back to his old self when I arrived home. I got a kiss on the cheek and he told me he was putting together dinner. He was a good cook, from his days of being a struggling actor and working in restaurants.

Out of a strong mix of curiosity, jealousy, and paranoia, I grabbed his cell phone off the coffee table while he was distracted with cooking. I headed to my bedroom for some privacy while I invaded his. Sitting on my bed, I shook as I scrolled through a history of interactions between Steve and the 25-year-old. Whatever narrative I had built about it being about the drugs and not about him... it was wrong. Overcome with the feeling I was going to be sick, I retreated to the bathroom and locked the door. I turned on the shower and hoped the sound of running water would cover the sound of my crying. What could I do? Skip back weeks? There was no timeline for me to go to where I wouldn't remember this, even if I could prevent it. After some time, I collected myself and headed downstairs, his cell phone in hand.

* * *

On December 24th, my plane touched down in Colorado Springs. It had been years since I had been in Colorado; my Mom had died a few years before while I was abroad shooting a movie. So, I'd spend Christmas alone. It was better that way; I was wretched company, and I couldn't imagine anyone putting up with me in my current state.

Beautiful white snow greeted me as I drove my rental car out of the airport. So much had gone wrong that week, but at least the snow was as it should be. It took me a short hour to make my way to Cañon City from the airport. I checked into the St. Cloud, a charming old brick hotel from the 1800s. The woman who ran it had been friends with my mom and wouldn't give me up. I didn't have a plan or know how long I was staying; I told myself I'd stay until I felt better.

The hotel had been renovated many times, once very recently. The St. Cloud looked different than I remembered, more modern maybe. My room had crisp white sheets and a black headboard on the bed, in addition to the dark wood and the blue and white area rugs. I opened the curtains to reveal a picturesque view of the mountains. Snow gently fell on downtown, and I felt justified in my decision to get out of LA.

Susan called then, and in her delicate way let me know that Steve had been photographed with the 25-year-old, and it was starting to make the rounds on social media. I wondered if the ink was dry on that Bond deal. Maybe Steve wasn't as smart as I thought. She asked me if it was over between Steve and me, and I said I didn't know.

After Susan's call I sat in the brown leather chair and stared out the window. What did I have? I was left with a career that wasn't fulfilling anymore, a big empty house, and my wealth. It should have been enough for me. It used to be enough. I had confronted

Steve about the cheating and told him I wanted to separate. That...wasn't how I usually handled things like that.

I started skipping around the age of seven, and I was used to the control and the freedom it gave me. Everyone experienced consequences for their actions; however, because of my ability, I hadn't had to live with most of mine. Skipping had let me take back the wrong thing I said, make a better first impression, and try things most people would avoid because of the consequences. But most people also learned how to temper themselves and their impulses. I wondered if there were some parts of me missing because I could skip. Maybe I was missing out on the human experience.

I had decided a long time ago to keep my time travel small. The natural question of course was, if I could time travel why didn't I do something for humanity? At that point in my life, my answer would have been this: for the same reason most people weren't in Doctors Without Borders. There are millions of problems in the world, and most people aren't giving any of their time to solving them. Why should I be expected to be different? That kind of time travel hadn't interested me, and it never seemed like something I could do on my own. There was a lot I didn't know about time travel and potential timelines, but what I did understand intimately was cause and effect. I was using skips mostly for my own benefit, but there were a few accidents I had prevented. I had saved two lives because of my skips, which felt like big events to me. I sure as hell wasn't going to press my luck by trying to affect something big.

At 4 p.m. I realized that I wasn't in LA but a small town in Colorado; if I wanted to get food other than room service, I sure as hell better get it before everything closed for Christmas. I bundled up and headed out of my hotel. Down the street I could see the glow of the sign for Murray's Saloon and hear loud, festive voices inside. I found myself drawn to the sounds and I stood outside for a bit, looking in to watch the people. My mood kept me from entering, so I kept walking. A short distance later I found a Thai restaurant that was open and next to them, with neon lights blazing, was the local pot shop, also open. Way to have priorities, Cañon City. I ordered enough Thai food for four people and then on a whim, I headed into the pot shop.

I didn't usually do drugs, not after my accidental LSD trip back in time. But I was cutting myself some slack today. Being out of control of my time travel was not something I ever wanted to repeat again, but I had done pot before without any "bad trip" issues. The people in the Thai restaurant hadn't seemed to recognize me, but the stoner working the pot shop definitely did. I got a couple edibles and resigned myself to the fact that come the next morning my hotel would be crawling with people wanting to get a photo of me, post-breakup.

The St. Cloud, or rather its bar, was bustling with people when I returned. A handsome man at the bar turned towards me and gave me an appreciative look. I gave him a nod and kept walking. Maybe someday, but not today.

I spent the rest of Christmas Eve eating Thai food and watching the snowfall. My sense of peace was shattered when a "forgive me" text arrived from Steve. Twenty minutes later he tried to call, twice. I muted my phone and reached for a pot cookie. I was having yet another panic attack, and I just needed to calm down.

My eyes closed, I laid on the floor of my hotel room and tried to take deep breaths. I didn't want to feel like this anymore. The hardwood felt oddly insubstantial to me, and I felt the equilibrium of my body shift, and sink into it, and then past it. Maybe I shouldn't have had the whole cookie. Beneath me, the floor was gone, and I could no longer hear the faint hum of the heater; my senses stopped relaying that I was in a hotel room. Opened my eyes, and I saw stars. Stars and interstellar dust, in every direction. I was standing up now, and I tried to understand what had happened. In the distance, I saw a bright light approaching. Or rather, I was approaching it. A river of blue light.

As I got closer, I realized that it wasn't just blue but made from many other colors—red, orange, purple, yellow. Like tiny threads of electricity running along a current, it flowed. I was looking at time; it was beautiful. The river seemed to go on forever, against a background of darkness and stardust. To my left, I noticed a shadow next to the river. The shadow moved and I recoiled, instinctively retreating back into myself. I had the sensation of falling. My stomach lurched as if I had changed direction suddenly. Then suddenly I was back, laying on the hotel floor. What was that?

* * *

On Christmas Day I woke up early and ordered room pancakes from room service. I grabbed my mug of tea and stared out the window to watch the snow fall, trying not to think about the fact I had so very few people to call on Christmas.

I had been time traveling for over thirty years and yet I knew so little about it. I didn't know why I could do it—certainly, none of the family members seem to have had that ability. At least, none that 'fessed up to it when I asked them when I was seven. After some consideration, I ate half a pot cookie and tried to find my way back to the river of light.

When I saw the time river again, the shadow was not there. After inspecting the river for a bit, I figured out what I was seeing in the light. To my left was the past and in front of me was the present.

If I kept following the river to my right, would I eventually find the future? From where I was standing it looked like the future went on and on forever, to a vanishing point.

My other discovery was that those small colors of light within the river were variations in time. I realized that one of those yellow variations I was looking at in 2017 was...me. I had prevented a car accident that saved a woman's life; and the yellow strand of time continued to my present. Were all those other color threads variations in time? I inspected a similar purple variation in time and found it unfamiliar. I felt a chill. I wasn't the only time traveler out there.

The next day, I was distracted by what I had seen at the river. Unless there were some sort of natural variations in the time-line, there were others like me out there. It was an intriguing and terrifying thought. How many of us would it take to create the variations I had seen? A dozen? Two dozen? Were all my skips visible in the river, or just the big ones? Most of the variations were small when compared with the magnitude of the river. If I could see variations in time from other jumpers, that meant they could see mine—someone could be watching me. I needed to find out more, so that evening I returned to the river.

Traveling was easier this time and when I arrived, there was a man standing next to the river downstream.

He was Asian and dressed in a classic style with a pair of brown slacks and a light blue button up shirt, the sleeves rolled up to his elbows. His face was serious and thoughtful as he examined the river, and I guessed that he was in his mid-30s. Finally, he looked up and saw me, a look of shock registering on his face. I guess he wasn't used to seeing people here.

"Hello," I said from a few feet away from him. At least sound worked in this strange place.

"Kon'nichiwa," he said, smiling.

"Hajimemashite," I replied.

A look of relief flashed on his face, and he replied in a flood of Japanese, none of which I could follow. I spoke enough Japanese for film press tours, which wasn't much. There were a few things I could pick out. His name was Yamato.

"Sumimasen, watashi no nihongo wa warui desu, (My Japanese is bad)," I explained in my halting Japanese.

He laughed and said, "Hai (Yes)." Well, then. Yamato apparently had a sense of humor.

We spent quite a bit of time there, trying to communicate. I was able to tell him my name, but not much beyond that. He didn't understand any of my English. Even so, there was an urgency to his demeanor. We were able to communicate that we should meet there again, but indicating time was impossible even though we could indicate the place.

Before we parted, Yamato grabbed my hand. "Daisaigai," he said steadily. He wanted me to remember that phrase.

"Daisaigai," I repeated back to him, and I nodded that I understood. That I would understand. He turned and walked towards the past and I wondered if I would ever see him again. I hoped so.

* * *

Daisaigai. *Catastrophe.* Yamato was trying to warn me of something.

The warning had given me a new purpose, and I was determined to communicate with Yamato. This would have been easier if I were physically traveling to the river. But this was a journey of the mind, and I didn't get to bring props. Which meant I needed to learn to speak Japanese. I installed an app on my phone and started lessons.

An hour in, Steve called me and this time I answered, ready to finally face my failed marriage. He wanted me back. I told him no. Maybe that was truly the first time I was able to see it; I had never even considered telling Steve about my ability to skip. What a thing to hide from someone. To hide from everyone. I said goodbye to Steve, effectively closing that chapter on my life.

It took four days and ten trips to the river to find Yamato again. He looked relieved as I was that we had met up again. In hopes of meeting him again, I had memorized a message in Japanese for him. I told him I was from 2019, and that I had found the river by accident. That I understood there was a catastrophe.

He nodded, "Arigatō gozaimashita (Thank you)." He seemed relieved to hear my Japanese but disappointed that I couldn't talk with him.

Yamato had also prepared something for me, in English. "Daisaigai. Hiroshima. Nagasaki. 1945," he said.

Dear God. Yamato waited, to see if I understood. Was Yamato from 1945? I thought about his style of clothes and the place next to the river I had seen him.

"Yamato, Hiroshima, Nagasaki, 1945?" I asked.

"Hai."

The United States had killed over a hundred thousand people

with those two World War II bombings. Did Yamato want to change that? Was that why he was at the river, examining it? He was still waiting for my reply.

"Hiroshima. Nagasaki. 1945. Daisaigai," I said, agreeing with him. "I'm sorry," I said finally. He may not know what I was saying, but I still needed to say it.

Yamato spoke more Japanese to me, but I didn't understand any of it.

" Ashita koko de aimashō (Meet me here tomorrow)," I said.

"Hai," Yamato said. Hands in his pockets, he walked away from me into the past.

I slept little that night, thinking about time and its consequences. How do you stop an atom bomb? And if you could, would something just as bad happen? Would human beings just inevitably start the next bad thing? Beyond questions of human nature and morality, there were logistics. I was born in 1980—could I travel back in time further than that? What would a jump to the 1940s mean for my body? It should be impossible. It might even kill me. But time was now a river to me, and there was still so much I didn't know. I wondered if Yamato had traveled back in time before his birth. Yet another thing I wanted to ask him about.

Thankfully, the next day I was relieved to meet Yamato at the river, right on time.

"I was afraid I would not be able to find you again," he said, smiling.

Oh, boy. "You speak English?" I asked.

"Yes," Yamato said. "It's been three years since I saw you last. I have been studying."

"It's been three years since we last met?" I asked.

"Yes. How long for you?"

"A day."

"I thought it would be better this way, and I also wanted to see what happened to Japan after the war was over," he explained. "Can I show you something?" He indicated I should walk with him, towards the past—his present—in the river. After walking for a while, he found the place he was looking for. He paused and indicated a part of the river. "This is when I am from—1949."

Something caught my eye downstream, in the past. I walked towards it to get a better look. Pieces were streaked in red, larger than the rest. It looked like the river was bleeding. "What is that?" I asked.

Yamato sighed, "That is Hiroshima and Nagasaki."

"You tried changing it by yourself since we last talked?" I had thought Yamato wanted my help in changing time.

"No, I changed it before I met you," he admitted. "But it did not work, not as I had hoped. I made it worse. Japan had also been working on an atomic bomb during the war, and developed it faster than the U.S. They bombed the west coast, and thousands of people died. Japan won the war. I did not want so many people to die, so I changed things. I went back in time to be at Hungnam to make sure they did not make the atom bomb. But the U.S. bombed Hiroshima and Nagasaki. I did not know they were close." he said with sadness when he reached the end of his story.

"I'm living in the time variation you caused by stopping Japan's atom bomb," I said. My future was one big variation, and not the original timeline.

"Yes. Changing the timeline had unexpected results. I understand many terrible things happened during the war. I need your help. You are from the future, and you may know more than I do. How do I stop this?"

"You want to stop the atom bomb from being developed?"

"Yes," he said.

"I don't know if we can. The problem is that someone will come up with it eventually," I said. "There's only so long you can stop the advancement of science."

"I have thought about this. If the bomb were discovered at a time of peace, instead of during a war, things might be different. Perhaps it would not be used," he suggested.

"Maybe," I said. "But what if we make it worse?"

Yamato turned to look at the river and said, "I have to try. This happened because of me and I must fix it. Maybe we do not need large change—just small things. Tell me, woman from the future—how do I keep the U.S. from bombing Japan?"

"Will Japan surrender without being bombed?"

"I don't know," Yamato admitted.

"Maybe preventing the technology from being developed is easier."

"We would have to know where they're building the bomb," Yamato said.

"We do. The Manhattan Project developed the atom bomb. It's in Oakridge, Tennessee," I explained. Yamato looked at me, surprised. "There's another thing about The Secret City in

Oakridge, Tennessee—they employed a lot of women, and I'd fit right in."

* * *

It's April 4, 2020 and we're in Paris, my favorite city and at my favorite time of year. Yamato leisurely reads a French paper while I sip my coffee. He looks very handsome, in his bomber jacket and blue button up shirt. My French is still better than his, so from time to time he asks me what certain words in the paper mean. Our conversation is a mix of Japanese and English—his English remains much better than my Japanese. Of course, he dedicated three years to learning English, whereas I have learned Japanese bit by bit, over the years.

Things haven't been easy, but of course we didn't choose this path because it's easy. We chose it because we wanted to make things better. The first few years were hard, until we started recruiting the others. We've dedicated ourselves to one hundred years of peace for humanity, and beyond that humanity is on its own. Yamato believes that if we can establish a few generations of peace and prosperity, people will set their expectations accordingly and maintain it themselves. I am less sure that people won't slide back into constant war and greed, but I have always been the less optimistic of the two of us. I think Yamato's early catastrophe with the timeline made him resolved to be its caretaker. His optimism and his idealism are why I fell in love with him.

Despite having seen the river of time, I think of time as a spider web. You pull on one strand and the shape of it changes. Pull on the wrong thread, and the whole web comes down. As we change one problem, we encounter another. Avert nuclearization, and the war goes on longer than in the original timeline. We saved a lot of lives and prevented a lot of suffering—wars, pandemics, natural disasters, climate change. But I'd be foolish if I thought that people weren't still getting hurt. There are always people we couldn't save. I never intended it to go this far—but once we started, it was impossible to stop. Time is a garden that requires constant care.

No one knows my name anymore and that makes me sad sometimes, but I have purpose now. The Paris newspaper tells me that Steve has recently gotten married to some beautiful young starlet. Of course, Steve and I never met in this timeline because I was never born. Something we changed in World War II caused it, and we're still not sure what it was. I don't exist in this new timeline, so there is no younger self for me to skip back to now. But I have made my peace with being missing from time. Yamato has an alternate version of himself out there, one that got married after the war and had children. I'm sure it's strange for him, but he rarely comments on it.

This is our life's work now—being guardians of the timeline. And in the meantime, in between figuring out time's puzzles, Yamato and I live our lives. I have purpose, and I have love. For some people, it might not be enough. But it is enough for me.

The Good Girl

Jennifer Lee Rossman

Jennifer Lee Rossman (any pronouns)
is a queer, disabled, and autistic author
and editor from Binghamton, New York.
Follow them on Twitter @JenLRossman
and find more of their work at http://
jenniferleerossman.blogspot.com

She was a good girl, and I miss her. God, do I miss her. Pastel sweet sixteen dress, whole life ahead of her, wholesome classic rock playing in the background as her blood was drained.

I miss her boyfriend, too, but he was too good, too stuck on the straight and hetero path to fall in love with the bad boy who woke up wearing her bloodstained party dress. Sometimes I think this would all be so much easier if he was still there for me.

But he got old and then he got dead and now he's buried under a cross not too far from the empty grave with her name on it.

* * *

I tried to be her. Tried to drink the blood of her friends who were still good, who were still girls, but it was too sweet for me and my body rejected it.

I even turned a couple of them, just to see if maybe immortality and puberty was as dangerous a mixture for them as it was for me. It wasn't, and now they're good girls forever, looking ahead at the bright future filled with eternal California summers spent obsessed with horses and fashion and boyfriends who love them enough to never get old and never get dead.

I was always told vampires hated sunlight and garlic. Not me. My sunshine was lipgloss, high heels my garlic.

So I tried to let her grow up. Let the good girl turn bad. I drank the blood of those trouble-making harlots in the short skirts that my Mama warned me about, but it was too bitter and it broke her heart to see me that way.

I had to let the good girl die. It was the only mercy I could give to those who loved her. I wish I could've given them a body to bury, if only because it didn't fit right anymore. Maybe never had.

* * *

The good girl was dead, but her ghost burned me like blessed silver no matter how I changed my appearance, my attitude.

It's a good thing I don't cast a reflection. Feeling like her was bad enough. Having to see her every time I looked in a mirror? Her curves, her face? I remember mirrors, remember their funhouse mockery, distorting me and making me face what the world saw when it looked at me.

I can't imagine an eternity like this.

* * *

I got reckless, because maybe I wanted someone to realize what I was and put a stake through my heart. Or maybe I just wanted someone to help me realize what I am.

He was a good girl. I thought so, anyway. But his blood tasted better, tasted right.

I'd had boy blood before, so refreshing. Too refreshing. I stayed away because I liked it too much, just like those girls my Mama warned me about back when I was still a good girl.

Or so I thought.

Did my blood taste like this, like the blood of a bad boy wrapped up in all the pastel ribbon trappings of a good girl?

* * *

She was a good girl, and I miss her, but she never really existed. She was neither good nor a girl; she was an act meant to please Mama, and the church, and that nice boyfriend who got dead and got buried next to the empty grave with her name on it.

The first time I changed forever, I didn't have a choice. Someone saw me, decided I was theirs to take.

This time, it's my decision.

I'm a bloodsucking monster, and I'm sure I'm breaking the hearts of everyone who ever thought they knew me, but I'm a bad boy and I'm done pretending otherwise.

The Silent Decades

Olga Kolesnikova

Olga Kolesnikova was born in Russia and lives in England. They write novels, short stories and poetry. They studied Creative Writing at Kingston University London, graduating with an MA in 2018. Their debut poetry pamphlet, Chronicology, was published by Sampson Low in the same year.

Anna D. Aclan, *The 21st Century: Before and After the Silent Decades* (York: New Capital Books, 2190)

NOTES

Part 1: 2001-2025

1. Josef J. S. Lane, *Fading into Silence* (Toronto: Modified Publications, 2175).

Katherine Utgaard, *The Silent Decades* (York: York University Press, 2168).

Lane considers the coming of the Silent Decades as a gradual restriction of communication culminating in a total ban. Utgaard's book argues for the more widely subscribed view of mass destruction of data during the War.

2. Oil-fuelled flight was the fastest form of long-distance travel, and the safest. It is estimated that over a million people would die in car accidents each year. For more information on this topic, see chapter 7 of Alyssandra Remond, *May We Meet Again: Deadly Travel Throughout the Ages* (York: New Capital Books, 2185).

3. Although the first half of the 21st century is known for its

controversially-named Petty Wars, I do not count this among them. See p.170 for a discussion of it as one of the causes of the War, as part of the Conglomeration Theory.

4. Countless similar attacks would occur leading up to and likely continuing into the Silent Decades. See Dante Lizar, *Stifled Cries* (South Monterey: Shifted Perspectives, 2181) for a (somewhat dramatised) detailed history.

5. Considering the highly controversial status of this facility prior to the War, it is easy to imagine the moral deterioration of governments that must have occurred to produce the dozens of similar facilities that emerged at the other end of the Silent Decades. This will be discussed in Part 2, but for more detailed information on these facilities, see Rachel Paul-Jansen, 'Descendants of Guantanamo' in *Detention: A Fragmented History of Imprisonment* ed. by Michael J. Nottingham (Vancouver: Chickadee Publishing, 2179).

6. Hannah Jordan, *Oil* (York: New Capital Books, 2179) – a fascinating and controversial history of petroleum, from the discovery of paraffin in the 19th century to the effective depletion of the Earth's oil at some point during the War. Most notably, Jordan boldly argues that, "the lives of our predecessors were tied to this substance–their suicidal tendencies grew with the onset of its extinction, and each leader was ready to bring down the world for a final gulp." (Jordan, p.330)

7. Casey Russo, *The Human Genome: A Sociocultural Disaster* (York: New Capital Books, 2185), p.115. Russo's work, first published in 2132, has since been met with severe criticism for her treatment of modified people as an unwanted by-product of the war.

8. Chike Oni, *The Invisible Continent* (Edmonton: United University Press, 2168).

9. The National Aeronautics and Space Administration. The rest of the country used a similar system of measurements, already outdated in most of the world.

10. Historians including Jasmine Hanton and Colin S. Goldman have argued that the European Union was a practical early model for the USW.

11. *Facebook*, 6 July 2170-present, New Capital Museum, York. The famous interactive exhibit allows visitors to browse millions of messages written during the final hours of the pre-War social networking site. This information was recovered during the ongoing *Internet Project*. A limited version of the exhibit is also available remotely.

12. Jerome Agne and Jamie He, *Duck Out of Water: How Environmental Weaponry Saved the Earth* (South Monterey: Shifted Perspectives, 2175). Agne and He argue that this and other natural disasters were test runs of environmental weapons later used during the War.

13. For a better understanding of American international interference, see Peter Schultz, *World Police* (York: Viking, 2168).

14. For a catalogue of species that went extinct during and around the Silent Decades, see Marie T. Chilwell, *The Way of the Polar Bear* (Aberdeen: Cults, 2184). Chilwell argues that while most of the 21st century's extinctions are believed to have occurred during the Silent Decades, the case of the Baiji and a fair number of others show that late pre-War human activity was already incompatible with the natural world.

15. "The Great Depression, the Great Recession – the greatest

of them all was yet to come, unnamed until its job was done."
Antonia Lucescu, 'Its Shadow' in *Post-War Poetry* (York: York
University Press, 2165), p.62.

16. *iPhones*, 6 July 2070-present, New Capital Museum, York.
Another exhibit in the museum's 21st Century Hall, this pile of
damaged and discarded personal communication devices is an
apt illustration of pre-War throw-away society.

17. Celia D. Huwlett, *Economic Models of the Past, Volume III:
Capitalism* (Edmonton: United University Press).

18. At this point, the world's population reached an unsustain-
able seven billion people. Such staggering statistics, along with
the tsunamis that later destroyed many of the world's major cities, gave rise to religious organisations such as the Second Flood,
whose members believe that the War was an apocalyptic event
caused by God.

19. The first nuclear meltdown caused by a natural disaster.
Agne and He discuss the post-War nuclear exclusion zones
likely caused by natural disasters (or environmental weapons) as
an unavoidable side-effect of environmental warfare but argue
that the effects of nuclear warfare would be far more devastating.
See the previously mentioned Jerome Agne and Jamie He, *Duck
Out of Water: How Environmental Weaponry Saved the Earth*
(South Monterey: Shifted Perspectives, 2175), pp.60-100.

20. Emmet L. Barnes, *Red Earth: From Curiosity to the Colonies*
(Edmonton: United University Press, 2183), p.12.

21. Janna Tones, *A History of Asteroid Mining*, (Saskatoon:
Saskatoon Publishing, 2180), p.351. It is regrettable that less
than a decade later, such promising scientific progress would
be stunted for over fifty years, and even then, required years

to recover. Katrina Stussy, The Unrealized Decades (South Monterey: Shifted Perspectives, 2187) is a fascinating exploration of the utopian possibilities of an imagined timeline where the War never occurred, and "the Silent Decades were unheard of; the years 2025-2078 were a golden age... a period of resolution and growth." (Stussy, pp.30-31)

22. This was not the first time the United States of America elected a television star – Ronald Wilson Reagan, the country's 40th president, was a famous actor prior to his political career.

23. For a better understanding of the destabilised condition of the United Kingdom's internal politics in the years leading up to the Silent Decades, see Dean Bexley, *The United Kingdom, 2010-2025: A Sociopolitical History* (York: York University Press, 2164).

24. Peter Smolov and Lisa C. Barker, 'Harnessing Gravitational Waves as a Power Source Using Orbital Graviton Farms', *United University Physical, Mathematical and Engineering Sciences Review*, 40.2, (2170), 201-350, (p.205). A century passed between Albert Einstein's general theory of relativity and the first confirmed detection of gravitational waves. The first graviton farm is predicted to be operational by 2230, meaning that humanity took over 200 years to realise a practical use for this energy source.

25. Killed using a high-precision Sarin gas bomb on the 17th of July 2022, just three days after the president's death. The bomb also killed four of his bodyguards.

26. For more detailed information on the particulars surrounding the assassinations, including the copycat theory, see Cristofer Jimenez, 'An Inspection of the Shared Circumstances

Surrounding the 2022 Leader Assassinations.', *World History*, 38.1, (2177), 3-58.

27. Claire L. Baker, 'Seoul and Pyongyang: The First Fallen Cities' in *Lost Cities of the 21st Century* ed. by Kathryn R. Chorley and Harry S. Wright (Toronto: Horizon Publishing, 2186), p.12. Baker's essay stands out from the rest of the collection as the two Korean capitals were destroyed just before the Silent Decades – for this reason, her essay is also by far the most factual and does not rely on conjecture.

28. Robert Malinky, 'The Extent of the 2024 Geneva Peace Summit's Success: Did the Nuclear Disarmament Agreement Prevent the Nuclear Apocalypse or Did the Removal of the Threat of Mutually Assured Destruction Usher in an Age of Environmental Weaponry?', *World History*, 43.3, (2182), 283-370.

29. Radiochemical analysis performed during the 2090s has suggested that the blast occurred somewhere between 2025 (the beginning of the Silent Decades) and 2030, leading to speculation that this was the event that triggered the Silent Decades and possibly even the War. For more information on the capital's destruction and a discussion of its effects, see Isaac Taylor, 'Washington, D.C.: Questions Raised by an Examination of the Irradiated Zone.' in *Lost Cities of the 21st Century* ed. by Kathryn R. Chorley and Harry S. Wright (Toronto: Horizon Publishing, 2186), p.116.

Part 2: 2078-2100

30. For most of the world, the Cognitive Awakening happened on the 7th of November 2078. However, records suggest that about 10% of the population experienced the phenomenon three days earlier. Initial claims that this 10% were modified

have since been debunked – the proportion of modified to non-modified was roughly the same as in the other 90%. See chapter 2 of Bruce Matthews, *The Cognitive Awakening* (Queenstown: Wakatipu Books, 2179).

31. Griselda Van den Berg and Joke Dekker, 'Amnesiac Effects of Solar Flares', *Psychoanalytica*, 2.1, (2080), 3-120, (p.43). This essay, excerpts of which were reprinted in all major newspapers as well as being widely broadcast, appeared to be the government's official stance on the cause of the phenomenon. Today, the essay's claims are largely viewed as a total fabrication.

32. For a more up to date view on the theory, see Joao Gamboa, *The Solar Flare: A Government Invention* (Toronto: Modified Publications, 2171).

33. Samantha Bell, *The Unsilenced Tribes: The Key to the Solar Flare Conspiracy* (Toronto: Modified Publications, 2185). This ground-breaking text was originally published in 2140. After decades of close, life threatening work with previously uncontacted tribes, Bell effectively ended the discourse on the validity of the Solar Flare theory with her revelation that none of the tribes uncontacted before the end of the Silent Decades had experienced anything like the Cognitive Awakening. Their lives seemed unaffected by the Silent Decades – they had memories and traditions that remained unchanged.

34. 'This substance's effects fell far short of the... 21st century's government's expectations... in concentrated doses, the agent's main effect is a *permanent zombification*... a totally compliant workforce' (my italics). From Gregory Kovacs, *Don't Drink the Water, Don't Breathe the Air: How the United States of the World's Government Erased Fifty Years of Human History* (South Monterey: Shifted Perspectives, 2184), pp.24-25.

35. Members of the Second Flood subscribe to the *Divine Intervention* theory, with a yet smaller minority believing the phenomenon to have been caused by intelligent extraterrestrial beings.

36. Muhammed Gamal, 'The 2078 Post Awakening World Riots', *World History*, 48.2, (2187), 228-278. Gamal refers to the aid effort as 'an unexpected moment of unity and a great sign of promise for the United States of the World, going forward.' (Gamal, p.228.)

37. Rosie Sherwood, *Yesterday was Fifty-Three Years Ago: Rediscovering Our Past* (York: Viking, 2180), pp.40, 122. Sherwood's book was originally published in 2099. Its merging of historical findings with poetic language has created a new literary genre and deserves to be read to this day. It is a personal favourite of mine.

38. Cassandra Silver, *Awaking Different: A Modified Mother's Memoirs* ed. by Strawberry Silver (Toronto: Modified Publications, 2166), p.72. Silver's memoir vividly captures not only the confusion of the Cognitive Awakening, but the slow shock of finding herself to be "abnormal." Like many modified people, Silver suffered from schizophrenia, which made it even harder to comprehend her situation: "it was impossible at times to accept myself as real." (Silver, p.20.)

39. For more information, see Janice Costo, *Inside Modified Communities* (York: New Capital Books, 2075)

40. Since the first edition's publication, my claim that the violence was propagated by plainclothes government agents among the peaceful protesters has been challenged. However, I stand by my claim; my research has been thorough and included an interview with Portia Benton, one of the last living participants

in the 2079 York protests, who has since sadly passed away. Furthermore, my findings were corroborated by Harry S. Wright, Alicia Penn, and Ross J.M. Osborn. My essay on this subject, published in *World History*, provides a more detailed look at the situation, which should extinguish any remaining doubts. See Anna D. Aclan, 'The 2079 York Protests and Their Effects: Government Involvement, Worldwide Outcry and the Freedom of Information.', *World History*, 49.2, (2188), 301-359.

41. This number is highly disputed due to the fact that the tsunami occurred before the investigation could be completed. See Emily L. Bryant, *The San Francisco Disaster* (Toronto: Horizon Publishing, 1974). Also Adreian Ramos, 'San Francisco: The Final Victim' in *Lost Cities of the 21st Century* ed. by Kathryn R. Chorley and Harry S. Wright (Toronto: Horizon Publishing, 2186).

42. "I've existed for 30 or so years, but I was born six months ago. Unlike you, I don't see an opportunity to start my life. I see a body that has been doing things without me for 30 or so years. In the mirror, I see a face as strange and frightened as those I pass on the streets. I see a 30-year-old corpse and I wish I had never awoken." Anonymous, in *Letters from the Post-War Suicide Wave* ed. by Jan Visser (Saskatoon: Saskatoon Publishing, 2179), p.87.

43. Some of the more notable publishers and journals formed as a result of this thirst for knowledge include *New Capital Books*, *Horizon Publishing*, and *Recovered History* (now World History) in 2079, *Jungle Publications*, *The General Scientific Review*, and *Chickadee Publishing* in 2080, and *Modified Publications*, *Viking*, *Political History*, and the *Biological Sciences Review* in 2081.

44. Philip Streep, *RCP* (York: York University Press, 2180), p.35. Streep's book is worth reading if you are interested in a comprehensive history of the Remote Communications Platform, from

its beta phase to what it is today. The book also includes a full discussion on the failure to reintroduce the Internet.

45. After a delay that dragged out into the next century, the project was finally abandoned in 2106. For a better understanding of the crushing effect of the project's failure, see Oleg Bezrodny, *The London Restoration Project: Giving Up on the Old Capital* (York: Viking, 2175).

46. This was also the first step in the Earth Cleanup Programme, completed in 2158. Despite the success of the mission, it was the only one of its kind. The risk of 'radioactive ash... enveloping the earth as a result of a failed launch is a very real possibility that could lead to our extinction.' Ned Bennet, '*The Nuclear Waste Expulsion Mission* as an Unrepeatable Achievement', *The Journal of Space Technology and Engineering*, 60.1, (2160), 60-110, p.67.

47. Winnie R.H.H. Athelstan, *The 22nd Century: Unsilenced* (Edmonton: United University Press, 2187).

Jinli Yu

Ai Jiang

Ai Jiang is a Chinese-Canadian writer and an immigrant from Fujian. She draws on cultures and landscapes of the lands she has walked for inspiration. Her work has appeared or is forthcoming in The Dark, Prairie Fire, Boneyard Soup, among others. Find her on Twitter (@ AiJiang_) and online (http://aijiang.ca).

Before they took you, we were watching the stream ripple as the gentle breeze caressed its surface. We tied our ox to a dove tree next to where we were sitting by the edge of the water. This was the time of day I loved most when you and I stopped by the river on our way home from a long day in the maize field during harvest season.

Though we work the land, we do not own it. And though we have private thoughts, we do not own our bodies. Huangdi owns all.

It was the first time you told me about jinli magic and the first time you showed me your true form. At that moment, father, you were more magnificent than Huangdì with your inked fins moving with the water, scales catching in the sun.

My feet dipped into the water, cool against sunburned skin, and drifted to the left from the pressure of the current. My fingers fiddled with my straw-weaved sandals tossed beside me. The water looked deeper, darker today. Your face looked overcast, though the sun had not yet started setting, and there were only a few clouds, but they were barely there and sat almost translucent against the blue of the sky.

You took off your clothes and folded them neatly, placing them beside me before diving into the rippling currents of the stream.

It was so sudden, I could do nothing but stare. My hands cold like the water. Your body morphed into one much smaller, magnificent white with black ink: a jinli. The magic intrigued me, but only for a moment, because with a sudden change the currents became too strong, too violent for you to swim against. It carried you away as you thrashed, or was it only pretend? Your fins disappeared in a flurry of white.

My bare feet kicked grass and dirt behind me as I scrambled after you. I stumbled several times over the uneven ground below the mountains. You told me that magic could not be used unless you are calm. I wondered if you were calm while you were carried away. And if you were, why did you not come back?

When you disappeared too far for me to follow, I returned to where your clothes lay and hid them in the bushes near the stream. You would need them when you find your way back.

I whisper into the water: *I wish for your safe return.*

* * *

You never taught me the jinli magic. How could I follow you?

I now return to the place where you left me and whisper daily into the water. I know there is little chance you can hear me, but the water always has its way of carrying a message. Water travels much greater distances than our bodies.

The villagers murmur about how Huangdi is paying high prices for those who can bring him jinli yu because jinli symbolizes wealth, power, bravery and such based on colour. I wonder, father, are you brave? You never told me what each of the colours means.

* * *

If someone found you and took you to the palace, you were no doubt fluttering under the waterfall, as you often do when you needed to be alone. You never noticed, but I always knew where you were because that is where mother disappeared.

You told me that jinli could swim up waterfalls, but only those brave enough, strong enough, determined enough. You are convinced that mother is at the top. I know this was not true, but you would not believe me. She could not be on the top of the waterfall because I saw her red-scaled body drifting downstream, luring the collectors away from you while I hid in the forest until you found me. We don't blame one another; we only blame ourselves.

Father, you cannot find her over the waterfall. But perhaps you already know and that is why you jumped into the water that day even though the currents were unsafe. Did you want Huangdi's collectors to find you?

* * *

The villagers tell me that the jinli festival will be hosted at the palace soon at the end of the year. Huangdi will release all the jinli yu he has collected in his pond. Jinli, the people like you and me. Will you return then?

I whisper to you again through the water, the trickle of the stream, the currents. My whispers are disruptions to the calm stillness in the middle of the night. I whisper my words to the currents in hopes they will carry my thoughts to you, but it is difficult when I am whispering upstream. The downward currents are unkind. But all the streams surrounding the villages lead to Huangdi's pond, though iron bars are blocking where the water flows outwards from the palace.

I return to our spot by the stream and place my clothes by yours in the bushes. My naked body cuts through the water, and I pray I am capable of magic before I hit the rocks at the bottom. I see the rocks and graze past them as the currents carry me downstream. Where others pray for opaque water to hide their colours, I hope, like my mother, I will be eye-catching enough to draw attention.

Wait for me, father.

* * *

You told me that no one is born free. Freedom cannot be earned, but often bought instead. True freedom, you said, does not exist. Are you free in the calm waters of Huangdi's pond? When will you forgo the calmness, the illusion of the calm, artificial pond and return to the irregular, rushing currents that carry you to the rest of us? The waters like the fields we tread against daily, feeling almost a sense of contentment in the struggle, rather than floating downstream with ease. For us, the struggle is normal.

When I think about your glassy eyes and inked scales when you disappeared, I understand why you never believed in true freedom. But unlike you, I believe it exists even if we must sacrifice our humanity for it, much like how Huangdi sacrifices his humanity for wealth and power.

You said what makes us different from the nobles and the royals is not our magic but our values: we value hard work, they value unearned wealth.

You told me that we become spirits when we can no longer turn human again. But even spirits must battle against the winds that threaten to carry them away.

* * *

When they find me by the waterfall, whispering the names of

both you and mother, I know I will meet you soon. But will you still be there, or will you have become a spirit?

* * *

As the festival continues and the nobles sway, drunk with wine. Our tails cut through the pond's still water. We make it look so weak compared to the rushing streams in the mountains. But this freedom feels false, unnatural, constructed. Unsatisfactory. Unearned. There cannot be freedom without the struggle. But father, you believe you have struggled enough.

I watch you swim, aimless, in the distance near a small water-fall. A waterfall that is hand-crafted rather than natural. It is smaller than the one you usually visit near the mountains. Your inked body thrashes against the current that is keeping you from climbing the fall while the rest of us dance in the calm water, not because that is what Huangdi wants to see, but we dance because we can. It is only during this festival where we can believe that we are somewhere else, someone else, even if it is only for a moment. And only a moment is enough.

Father, why do you struggle to remain the same, but in a different place?

* * *

When the festival concludes, all the jinli yu, including myself, gather by the iron bars where the pond connects to the outer streams. With a booming laugh, Huangdi calls for the guards to open the pond gates. I now understand that he does this only so he can catch us again the following year when we most desire rest; when we no longer desire to swim against the current.

Without effort, the downwards current pulls us along the stream once we are outside the palace walls. I turn back and catch sight of you, still trying to swim up the hand-crafted waterfall. Alongside the other villagers, I leave you behind. Once a safe distance away from the palace, each jinli transforms back into their human forms and climbs out of the water one by one. They wave to the rest of us after fumbling to pull on the clothes they hid.

Father, you cannot stay at the palace forever.

* * *

I lean back on my hands at our usual spot by the stream with my feet cutting through the calm water. It has been almost a year since the festival, and I have been hard at work, harvesting the crops in the maize fields. The crops that you left behind, do not worry father, are thriving.

* * *

The festival is approaching again. The palace men take my harvests to Huangdi, leaving me with only enough to survive. Sometimes, I think about the jinli magic, and you under the waterfall at the palace, but I know I will not hide my clothes by yours and enter the water again.

No matter what jinli I had become last year, our magic is only meant for a temporary rather than permanent solution to our daily, mundane battles. We cannot swim up waterfalls with magic alone.

Perhaps next year, you will return. *And father,* I whisper into the water, *I will wait at the top of the waterfall.* Turns out mother is already there like you said, but only you, father, could never figure out how to get there. You were never be brave enough to let go of the past. No matter how hard you swam against the rapids of the fall, you made not progress. To find mother, we have to let her go.

When I raise my face from the water, I see a dragon jinli yu with swirling colours symbolizing bravery, strength, and determination, dancing where my reflection should have been.

Soon, I will join mother on top of the waterfall, while you, father, continue to flutter at the bottom.

Elixir of Life

Amy Bennett

Amy lives in Australia, where she spends her time between postgraduate study and lighthearted creative pursuits on the side. She likes stories that tug on the threads of fantasy, sci-fi, or anything just a little magical.

Murders didn't quite draw the same crowd as they once did. Although it was no secret that everyone on the Black Agora Space Station didn't have the time to dawdle. Instead, they were down at the docks bartering for a ticket to a third-generation colony planet or a backwater moon—to anywhere but here.

Everyone except me, I supposed, with an ugly twist of my mouth. It was the kind of face my mother would tell me to straighten out, fingers tipping up my impertinent chin. But she wasn't stuck on clean-up duty in the Sita District slums now, was she?

No one else could do the damn job, anyway. Even if private eyes weren't so welcome in a city overrun by criminals; drug shipments and gang wars rolling in and out, soaking the ground like the crust of sea foam on waves of exhaust. Yet, those treacherous airwaves had to break apart on someone, anyone, who stood against the tide—and that was where I came in. Detectives were the only law worth the hassle, most of the time.

If you weren't spending your last days choking on fumes or shaking with an elixir addiction, it wasn't so bad. The largest intergalactic port in the galaxy had its moments of quiet, between that hum of spaceboats and haggling in the marketplaces, where the noise was beaten down, as thin and oily as the credits that slipped between greased hands.

It was kinda pretty, too. Maybe. If you stared up at the grimy fluorescents that hovered over the length of the space station, it looked like a rind of blue moonlight, almost. Or what I could guess it looked like.

Huffing, I shook my head. Hopefully that would help clear my mind. Crouching down beside the corpse, I pulled the cigarette from my lips in a pinch of my fingertips. My hand ached, limbs sluggish after a sleepless night, fighting to let some bad tasting hooch pull me into oblivion. Flecks of orange ash fluttered to the ground.

"Who was it that wanted me to find you so bad?" I asked aloud. In my right eye, I scrounged through the projected blue screen of my optical receiver to find the answer. The holographic text and image shuddered, light flashing like a comet streaking through the starry sky.

The first message in my inbox had the attached subject line of I NEED YOU.

CARINA PANDORUS MAJOR,

THERE IS A JOB FOR YOU JUST OUTSIDE GOZLEME'S CORNER SHOP, 17TH QUADRANT, NORTH SITA DISTRICT. BE THERE IN THREE HOURS. SECOND HALF OF PAYMENT TO BE RECEIVED UPON COMPLETION.

I'd taken worse tips, and for much less. The hefty sum of Universal Credits that was promptly deposited into my bank when I opened the message had made the investigation a whole lot easier to accept, even if I didn't really have a choice in it.

I gave the job—that poor sucker lying broken on the ground—a quick once-over.

At first glance, it was an open-and-shut case: a victim of elixir overdose. He had track marks bruised into the bend of his elbows, but his teeth were unblemished. His fingernails were a healthy pink. Somehow a good, clean man had been made to look like a drugged-out wretch.

I rubbed the bruised skin beneath my eyes. Sometimes I wondered if I pressed down too hard it would split open like the flesh of a fig, pulled apart to reveal the soft insides. My dad would buy three of the same fruits at the tail end of the Earthtime harvesting season; one for each of us in our family. It'd been so long that I'd damn forgotten what they tasted like, though. Not a lunar cycle went by when this place didn't make me hate it just that little bit more.

With as much finesse as a local meat butcher, dirty-fingered hands as big as cleavers, I dug out the victim's right eye to scan his optical receiver. Light flooded my mind in bursts, like the first initial jolt into hyperspace in rickety Earthtime spaceboats. I found his name and personal details. Alexei Chernyshevsky had a wife, five kids, and a life cut too short. Proceeding his refugee status from Janus ALPHA-7 was Chernyshevsky's high-clearance workman certificate.

I smirked; laughter squeezing out between my clenched teeth. There was only one company on the whole station that legally granted full travel and transport rights between the districts of Sita and Rama. Titan Corporation was the only place rich enough to buy that kinda privilege.

A siren filled the overcrowded, polluted atmosphere above my head. I straightened up to full height, windswept coat clinging to

my ankles like the wet crust of garbage underfoot. The police—
men recruited and churned out into government issue cyborgs
called Tinmen—didn't much like me shouldering in on their
turf, but there wasn't much trouble unless I was caught. Well,
thereabouts.

I rolled my neck until it cracked, ready to face whatever trouble
that came a-knockin'.

* * *

"Theia Titan. A pleasure to meet you."

I knew I was in danger the moment I saw her. Long legs, bright
eyes that weren't shadowed by the constant dim, and a knowing
quirk to her mouth that made my stomach twist painfully. Like
being gutted, except worse, because it's her hand I wanted pulling that part of me undone. I cleared my throat, forcing myself to
look at the full splendour that was Theia Titan.

She was as polished and cold as the stars that shined above. Just as
beautiful, too. And she was also the unofficial kingpin of Agora.

If you were stuck long enough on the space station, you were
quick to learn there was a basic hierarchy on the streets: Titan
Corporation, Tinmen, and gangsters. They all managed to keep
the place in such a state of drugged-out, boozed-up chaos that it
seemed we were all living through the same maddening night
without end. Without a sun to guide ourselves by, it was just
about true. Instead, we had a synthetic version of light; it was
just another bad copy of the real thing.

"Carina Major, was it?" Theia stood facing me, her slender
profile outlined by the illuminated landscape of Agora behind
her. Light spilled over her bare shoulders, molten, like gold, or a
supernova collapsing in on itself. Her office was made entirely of

glass, so delicate and clean I couldn't believe it was only just me and her up there.

Another piece of me, low in my body, was wrenched out.

"Yes, ma'am."

"Is that an accent I detect?" She folded her hands behind her back, watching me with interest. Her mouth pressed into a thin line, the purple lipstick almost the same colour of those figs I had when I was a kid. I wanted to know if they tasted the same. "An early generation colonist's daughter who went off searching better things and got stranded here, perhaps?"

"I'm here to speak with you about the recent death of your employee, Mr. Alexei Chernyshevsky." I strained to keep my expression neutral, my shoulders up. Gaze forward.

She was already having too much fun with me.

"Is this an interrogation?" Theia asked, moving to stand behind her desk. They were slow, measured strides.

"It's just procedure. Did Chernyshevsky have any complaints, workplace disagreements, or anything that would lead you to believe someone had the motive to—"

"Kill him?" Low laughter echoed eerily in the glass room. "No, Mr. Chernyshevsky was a model employee. I had no qualms with the man." Theia paused, her lustrous hair half-shadowing her face, like an Earthtime temple goddess shrouded in the muck of grime and disuse. "However, wouldn't you say this is a matter for the police?"

I swallowed thickly. I was starting to understand why I was even allowed up here; it wasn't a trick I'd learned from years throwing around my weight as a private eye. "With all due respect,

Tinmen aren't much help most of the time. I'm the best chance an innocent man has at finding justice."

Theia snorted; it was just a small, soft thing. She did it in the same way a classy dame sneezed delicately behind a cupped hand. Unease drew my mouth into a frown at her show of lady-like fragility, so completely at odds with how she spoke, shouldering in, demanding to be heard and obeyed.

"I feel like a cigarette," Theia said suddenly. "Would you like one?"

"Mrs. Titan—"

"White Hare, wasn't that your brand?"

I took her up on her offer, knowing it would be better to play along. Across the space of the desk, we leaned into each other. Like the flimsy edges of the space station, reaching out to touch, leaving only a desperate longing in its place. Funny how being so close to her, alone, was more frightening than dodging the elixir-drugged masses that congregated down below. That I could handle, at least.

Theia waited until I had taken a slow drag of the slim, black cigarette, mouth touching the place where hers had been, before responding. "I would talk to the families that run Sita District," Theia said. "They've never quite taken to me, for whatever reason."

I nodded tightly, recording the information on my optical receiver. I didn't have the luxury to wonder if she had the tech to track my internal actions. Be lucky if she didn't lace that cigarette with anything, even if she shared it with me. I had my money on her having built up a resistance to poison, though, after surviving—and succeeding—in Agora this long.

"Please contact me if you have any other questions," Theia called out as I made the motions to leave, quick to escape a feeling I didn't really wanna analyse right now. "And you should know it's *Ms.* Titan. My late husband has only just recently left this world, the poor thing."

* * *

There was a strip of neutral ground between the Sita and Rama Districts where any weary soul—be it human, android, or alien—was free to do as they pleased. It was the only place I could bribe my informants to meet me without worrying about who would report back. It wasn't worth breaking the one truce people stuck to outside those boundary walls.

And no one wanted to remember what they did in Purgatory, anyway.

"You heard of Alexei Chernyshevsky?" I asked the two men eating at a street-side noodle stall. The constant motion of the kitchen blew steaming humidity in face, so hot that I swore my skin was sloughing off in sweaty layers. Hard to imagine what it actually felt like to burn—the sun here was barely functioning lightbulbs, producing a sickly glow.

"What'd the guy do?" Sergio asked, leaning over Kenji's shoulder to talk to me.

"He was a Titan employee, workman certificate and everything. Killed in Sita District this morning and pumped full of elixir to make it look like an overdose."

My foot bounced impatiently against the ground as Kenji made a noncommittal grunt, laying his chopsticks across the top of his bowl. Sergio followed up his companion's act by slurping on the noodled entrails left in his watery broth.

What a perfect pair they were: silent and stupid.

"I don't have all day to entertain small-fry gangsters like you two." I planted my elbow on the bench, cocking my head. I wished I hadn't spent an asteroid-sized chunk of Universal Credits on paying for their meals when all I really wanted was a smoke. Preferably held between Theia Titan's elegant fingers.

"Cool your thrusters, Major! Here, have a drink," Sergio suggested, pouring a fresh glass for me. He slid it over, fingerprints imprinted on the glass messily. I could read his DNA with my optical implant if I really wanted to bother with scanning it.

My shoulders sunk; a sigh draining all the energy from my body. I stared at the amber-coloured swill for a while, but my self-preservation was short-lived. It hit the back of my throat like a metal-boned bruiser's fist and burned all the way down.

"Chernyshevsky was a Tinman," Kenji said without working up to it, still refusing to look at me.

"Been undercover for about two Earthtime years," Sergio added.

I frowned. "What would the gangs get out of killin' a rat in Titan Corporation?"

Kenji and Sergio halted, sharing a meaningful look I couldn't read. Even if they did serve on opposite turfs, information swirling in different mouths, gangsters knew how their own kind ticked. Something about being from the same cloth—as an old, elixir-ridden pioneer colonist had once told me. Kinship ran deeper than blood and wires around here.

"Who gave you that idea, boss?" Sergio laughed, thumping his chest as it caught in a hacking cough. He knocked his bowl as he did it, spilling it over the bench.

I cursed, sinking napkins into the chicken bone broth until they were coloured brown. Sergio was still making a racket, face flushed. Eventually, Kenji took pity on him for damn near spewing up blood and reached out to pat his back comfortingly. The strangled sound eased.

If I really focused, I'm sure the whole world would've narrowed down to a few singular things: Sergio's coughing; the scrape of a wok against a nearby stovetop element; and Kenji's hand slipping up to brush a thumb over the curve of Sergio's neck, just under his hairline. Purgatory had that affect—it made everything lose its harsh edge, just for a second. I could pretend I was in any other Earthtime shop, idling away the day, like I did when I was a kid. Like I stopped doing when I realised I had no idea what to dream about.

"Titan killed Chernyshevsky," Kenji said, in almost a murmur. I could barely hear him—always the damn noise, too loud and too close. "It wasn't anyone who worked this side of Purgatory."

"Why?" I asked right as my head started aching. I blinked, but my vision was getting dangerously hazy, like most nights I wanted to scrub out from behind my eyelids. Swearing, I tried to stand, tripping over my stool. "What did you do to me?"

The hot steam fluttered the fabric signs draping over the overhang of the noodle stall. It had gone quiet, weirdly, in that way silence pulsed after a tinny gunshot.

Sergio and Kenji's gazes slid to each other, like they always did. Like they always had—in sync. Hate swelled up inside me, bitter, like an off-world drink that had sat too long in a dinky hooch rig. Kenji slung his and Sergio's coats over his elbow, tugging Sergio to his feet.

I struggled to grab for them, wanting to demand an answer, help, *anything*.

– You pay decent, but we know folks who pay better," Sergio said, the words strained, scraping against his raw throat. He seemed faraway. "Chernyshevsky saw something he shouldn't have. He deserved better, but I guess he couldn't keep playing a lucky hand forever."

"But—" I gasped, choking. "He's a Tinman. Had protection."

"Don't you get it, Major?" Sergio's laughter lost its usual warmth. I wouldn't know—I barely felt the heat of anything beyond the burning warmth of Theia's eyes on me. "The Tinmen *are* Titan."

* * *

I woke up to the unwashed swill of my dirty mouth, sinking into the back of my throat. Stupidly, I wondered if cyborgs could taste their own blood when they had the snot beat out of them. I didn't know if it had been Sergio or Kenji, or even another two-bit gangster, to do the job, but whoever it was didn't hold back.

I groaned as I pushed myself up into a sitting position, pain flaring through every part of my body at once. There was a strange lucidness to how I moved when my nerves weren't drowned in the hazy smokiness of liquor. Pain throbbed at the centre of my awareness. Wincing, fingers pressed gingerly over my fragile human ribs, I ground a moan out between my cigarette-stained teeth.

It fucking hurt to feel so much.

I dared to open my eyes—my left was so swollen it wasn't even getting any readings from my optical receiver. I could see, barely, that they'd pulled me into an old warehouse to work me over, which I would've appreciated if not for the small, purple-tinted vial protruding from the bend of my arm.

The bastards had run elixir through my system. In two hours, I'd be energised, have quicker reflexes, and look almost ten years younger. By six, I'd either be feeling like I wielded the power of an ancient Earthtime god or gnawing through the bloody stump of my own tongue. Life or death—that was the game. It wasn't a drug that did things in halves.

I reached into my jacket, hoping for a break from this nightmare. But my fingers met an empty pocket, skating across crumpled menthol packets. Except, there, I could feel something lost in the folds, fragile and forgettable.

It was the cigarette Theia had given me. I stared at the purple stain of her lipstick on it, feeling the muscles of my face forming something as gruesome as a smile. I wondered if it would taste like figs if I put my mouth over the same place that she did. Beneath the lovely mark of colour, I found an innocuous strip of white.

I dug out the piece of paper, thinner than the sharpened tip of a syringe. My heartbeat thrummed beneath my skin, louder and more alive than it had ever been. I blinked, rapidly.

The message read:

Meet me where the lovers touch.

* * *

Black Agora Space Station was shaped like a crescent moon, the ends of it curled so close together they almost touched. At both opposite points of the Sita and Rama Districts, named after old

Earthtime lovers, it's said you could reach out to touch the other side if you stretched far enough.

Theia was waiting for me at the farthermost edge of Rama, where it was blocked off from the public under the wrong weather conditions. Although I don't think I'd ever be with Theia under the right circumstances.

I walked up the steep slope to the lookout, footsteps coming down heavy, the force of movement rattling my bones.

"You killed Chernyshevsky, didn't you?" The words felt large and clumsy in my mouth. My body was already reacting, veins pulsing and skin damp. There was poison in my blood, purple like my father's bruised figs, like Theia's stained lips.

"Well, it wasn't me, exactly."

"Just answer the fucking question!" Time wasn't a privilege I was allowed.

Theia turned to gaze across the whole laid out sight of Agora, spaceboats and slums and stars all jammed together. I wished, senselessly, that I could see her expression then. Halfway dead and all I wanted to know was what a pretty lady was thinking.

"Chernyshevsky was just in the wrong place at the wrong time."

I waited, hoping there was more. I didn't want this to end.

"You see, my dear Carina, my company is developing the cure to end all suffering. Yet that required a hypothesis that needed to be tested." She stepped closer to me, so close we almost shared the same breath. I'm sure I could taste the poison on her lips if I pulled the air deep enough into my quivering lungs.

Theia—or me, too—was always playing that damn game of

getting closer to the thing that could kill you, daring it to make the first move.

"Look," Theia whispered, revealing the smooth expanse of her arm. Air hissed through my teeth as I saw the ruined shape of her skin, bearing a pockmarked history of drugs. They were precise marks, piled on top of each other until the skin couldn't heal, ripping apart. Scabbing over. Torn again and again and again.

"Immortality is not such an attractive venture now, is it?"

Elixir. The old Earthtime myth of a potion to grant eternal life.

"Titan engineered elixir and released it into Agora to... test its effects?" I was starting to pant in ugly heaving breaths. The weight of clothes on my shoulders dug into my skin. "The deaths, the addictions—all that was your doing?"

Theia smiled, the corner of her lips curling up. "My decision to hire you was not unfounded, I see."

I blinked. "What?"

"It is a perfect set-up, isn't it?" There was that same voice, caressing the words, slow and sweet as a knife snuck between the ribs in a lover's embrace. "Your DNA on Chernyshevsky's body; an untraced amount of money in your account; recorded contact with me upon his death. It's obvious you were blackmailing him for inside information, and once he took his own life you turned your attention to me."

I fumbled for my gun, unable to aim it at Theia without shaking. Elixir had made me a shambled mess of failing parts, like a decommissioned Tinman sent out for scrap. I could taste the metal in my hands. My stomach was unravelling like a string pulled from a broth-soiled shirt sleeve. The colour of the sky seemed so impossibly heavy then, like it could crash down over my head, shattering into a million glittering glass shards. It was a fantasy that couldn't hold up.

"So, my dear Carina," Theia said, pulling her own black, compact pistol on me. "This is our tragic end, I presume?"

Theia's eyes shone brightly, even in the perpetual darkness of night-time. But the light of distant suns was still a cold, awful thing, after all. Agora didn't know what true warmth was.

"It was a pleasure to meet you."

As a shot rang out, deafening in its finality, my gaze dropped to stare at the lovely purple smear of Theia's mouth.

Look to the Future

Louise Hughes

Louise is a speculative fiction writer
whose work has previously appeared in
Strange Horizons, Daily Science Fiction
and Interzone.

I was sixteen-years-old when I realised that I couldn't see the future. The teacher held me back after the lesson finished. She was confused, disappointed even. I'd never sat in her classroom and refused to write on the page when asked.

"I know the future can be scary," she said, leaning against her desk with her glasses on her head. "Is there something that's worrying you? You know you've still got time. University applications don't have to be in until January."

I shook my head. I did not understand.

What followed was a series of tests, questions asked and unanswered. Four months later, they declared that no, I could not see into the future.

"But how is that possible?" my mother asked.

"It's rare but not unknown. Some people just don't seem to be able to."

"But how can she make the decisions she needs to make?" my father asked. "How can she have a future if she can't see it?"

"There are techniques we can look into. I'll give you some contacts."

After that, no one wanted to ask me to decide about anything. Little things, of course, like what to eat. As children we had made those decisions on an impulse. Let's go out this weekend, into town. Let's go and see that film that's on, that everybody's talking about.

But as adults, decisions are taken with far more care. Have you checked if town will be busy this weekend? Have you checked if the film is popular enough that we won't get there and find we should have bought tickets? Why did you go in the shower when you knew the phone was going to ring?

"Just let me have a look," my mother said when I suggested anything. She felt obliged to look into the future for me and declare it safe to go there. I sat down on the stairs to put on my shoes, shoving my feet in so hard my toes slammed against the ends. I pulled the laces tight, knowing I'd have to slacken them on the bus.

"I don't care."

I went to a Future Thinking workshop, at the doctor's suggestion and with great enthusiasm from my parents. As if by going through a series of meditation steps and making bullet-point notes, I could learn to see the future the way everybody else did. I saw excitement in their eyes. They drove me down there instead of letting me catch the bus.

Six weeks later, I still couldn't see into the future. We agreed I would stop going. They were quiet for a week but I was glad to stop spending two hours of every Saturday trying to push a rock up an icy mountainside.

I overheard them from the bathroom, after they thought I was fast asleep.

"What kind of future is she going to have if she can't see it? What are we going to do?"

One Friday after school near the end of the summer term, me and Kat went back to hers with pick-and-mix and raided her DVD collection. The rest of our friends had caught the bus out to Westburn Park to shop for the holidays and for the beach. I had never enjoyed shopping but these days hangers were held up and decisions made on flashes of the weeks to come. They all knew already if we were in for a dry and blue sky six weeks off.

"What's it like?" Kate unravelled a strawberry lace above her face.

"What?"

"Not being able to see what's coming."

I shrugged. "Don't you remember when you couldn't?"

"Not really. Is it just, like, darkness?"

They don't really understand. "It's not that I can't *see* the future. It's more, like, I have no way of looking. I don't know where to start."

The tail of the lace dangled from her mouth as she chomped. "Maybe you're just not old enough yet. You know, like periods. Everyone gets to it at different times."

"Aye, maybe."

When I was seven, I wished that it was Christmas already, closed my eyes, crossed my fingers, tried with every fathom of me to make my wish come true. When I opened my eyes, and the trees and lights weren't up, I didn't conclude that wishes didn't work. That would be silly. I believed in magic. No, I decided that must mean that Christmas would never come. I couldn't jump into a future that was doomed to never happen.

Christmas came, of course. But as I sat back against Kat's sofa, peeling flying saucers off the roof of my mouth with my tongue, I wondered if the reason I couldn't see the future was that the future wasn't coming.

The future came, like Christmas. I made my decisions about my future with reckless abandon. Everyone worried. They narrowed their brows and clenched their teeth and fretted that I was making a Terrible Decision that would Ruin My Life Forever. How could any choice I made be right? I couldn't see the future.

"I'm going to be a marine biologist," Kat had declared in Year Five, wrapped up in our big woolly scarves in the playground. She had to explain what both of those words meant. As the summer term of our sixteenth year ended, she did not tell me what her plans were. I had to ask.

She hesitated. "I've applied to study geology. I get much better results. My chances of a first in that are really high. Even top of the class a few times when I looked."

After a month of crippling indecision, late nights, shouted arguments and abject, paralysing terror, I applied to study history. We went to tours of universities and the beaming student guides declared, "I'm sure you can see you'll be happy here". Everyone nodded, smiling and content. They really could. After the third instance of this, we stopped taking tours and I picked my university based on size, and the ratio of flowers and trees to concrete.

No one believed I'd made the right decision. I started second-guessing myself within hours of sending the confirmation. And when I didn't learn to see the future in that first semester, everybody sighed and just knew: they'd been right.

When I came home for Christmas, I met Kat at Midnight Mass, both of us wrapped up tight against the chill of thousand-year-old stone. She gave me a card for my parents and I gave her one from mine.

"I'm not coming home in the summer," she said. "Good luck, you know, with everything." She could not see me in her future anymore. As I walked home through the slush and rain, I tried to look into the future. I could not see myself there either.

That was the year my granddad died, seven months after a wracking cough. We all saw it coming. The minister said "I'm sure we can all see a time when things will feel less painful than this", and no doubt this was meant to be a comfort, but she was wrong. The years ahead, to me, were empty. No matter how many times my mother looked ahead and knew that I would be there. I watched her, sitting at the kitchen table with her cup of tea and magazines, and wondered how far the future full of her extended. I couldn't look. I couldn't prepare. I returned to university by train and cried to myself in a seat going backwards beside the window.

I was twenty-one when I discovered I could see into the past.

I'd spent a particularly miserable day at the library, trying to break down my reading lists and prioritise. It baffled me how everyone else seemed to get through it all while I got through none of it. There just wasn't time. I had to read everything. There was no way of knowing which things were most likely to come up in that week's seminar. Each week the reading built-up. Each week I looked down the list and knew, just knew, I couldn't get through it.

So I didn't try.

I spent whole days doing nothing and now, here I was, nearing the end of the semester with eight weeks of reading still to do.

As I sat at the desk in the quietest corner, watching everyone else intent on their work or taking a break they somehow could afford to take, I did something I hadn't done for years. I closed my eyes and tried to see the future.

I let myself think, for a moment, that maybe I just hadn't been trying hard enough.

That was when it happened. A flash, an image flickering around me even though my eyes were closed. I thought, in a brief giddy moment, that I was doing it, that finally it had come to me. The ability to see into the future. My entire life shifted in that second.

Then I saw it again and realised that wasn't true. What I saw wasn't the future. It wasn't the seminar and the direction it would take or the first weeks of summer in pouring rain. I saw, with brief but perfect clarity, a vast room filled with machines, hammering away in silence, spinning, spinning. Women stepped forward with each swishing retreat of the machines, children dived beneath the net of cotton.

I opened my eyes and knew. That was the first time I saw into the past. It wasn't a grand event, no Waterloo or Agincourt, or shouting crowds in protest. It was a mill in dark autumn, rain lashing silent against the windows. It flickered. I couldn't focus on detail but I could seize the atmosphere, the busyness, and capture it.

Things got a little better after that. Not with the reading list. That was doomed. But after one excited phone-call, in which

I told my parents what I could do and they asked what was the good of that, I stepped back regularly.

I sat in the exam, read the question, closed my eyes and went there. I saw. I knew. It brought back a passion I thought those first ten months of learning crushed.

From then on, I had something no one else did.

I was twenty-six when I met someone else who couldn't see into the future.

Beth hid it better than me. She knew the answers to give and she'd mastered the art of making decisions based on emptiness. She told me not to fear the future just because I couldn't see it and we spent the summer climbing mountains. No one but us thought it was a good idea.

"I just don't know if you'll be happy," said my mother.

"Be careful, just be careful," said my father.

As all around me, my friends and acquaintances gathered together for marriages that lasted decades.

"We're going to have three children. Any more and they won't get along. Any more and we won't be able to give them our full attention. We have seen it. We will be so happy together."

I looked back, at all the centuries of happiness and joy, of people just being people, together.

One day, not long after we'd met, Beth asked me what attracted me to history and I took a breath and told her. I hadn't told any-one before. I thought maybe they'd accuse me of cheating, even though every one of them looked forward for the direction their studies should go.

I explained, and she understood as no one else did, how hard it is to find enthusiasm for something that might never happen. For something we couldn't see. The future? It's meaningless. It doesn't exist. But the past. That's there. I can see it, in glorious rainbow shades no photograph can convey. Deep purple knitwear, delicate cornflower blue embroidery, red hair. I sat on a train once, waiting on a bridge outside the station, while everyone around me collected their baggage and text-ed their homes to say they were coming. I looked down the river, saw the banks on either side, the other bridges vanishing to a time before they were built. Smoke and ships and cranes.

"I remember the day, the minute, where exactly I was sitting, when I really truly realised that the streets a hundred years ago weren't black and white. Seeing it made it true."

Beth didn't try to do it at first. We hadn't known each other long and perhaps she still didn't believe me. It was a few years later, when we'd got a house with separate offices, two cats, and a whole set of matching crockery, that she learnt to do it too. She found one of my photographs in the front room, dropped from the folder after an evening of book edits.

She asked me about it and after letting me unspool my knowledge for twenty full minutes she nodded and closed her eyes.

She needed to know where to begin looking. History is vast and it's helpful to know where you're aiming for.

The useful thing about it was she saw things I didn't. Even me, focused on detail, seeing everything around me, apparently didn't see everything in the past. It was a matter of experience. Beth looked for different things, in different places.

After that, I hesitate to say, we were unstoppable.

One summer, in the Alps, we bumped into Kat. I'd heard dribs and drabs, of course. She'd done well in geology as she knew she would. She worked for an oil company and travelled the world.

"No one with you?" I asked.

She shook her head. "I'm happy on my own." She had seen it.

"We should meet up for coffee, or something, back home."

"I don't go back much."

Her parents worried. They had seen her all alone and that was not how things were supposed to be. They fretted. They asked if she wasn't missing something, not looking hard enough. I tried to be sympathetic but how could I be? She didn't see me in her life. She saw she would be happy. Both of those things, to her, were irrefutable. They were the future.

I was thirty-three years old when the future fell apart.

We knew something was wrong when the screaming started, the wailing through the walls and doors. People in their streets and homes, one by one, looked forward and saw only grimness. It didn't matter what they tried, which future they tried to see. They stopped looking. They were too scared.

Our neighbour, a man with two cats, lived alone because his partner worked at a university in Ireland. We went around and knocked on his door and found him sitting on the settee with his head in his hands.

"I don't understand," he said.

Beth sat on the floor in front of him. "What's happening?"

"I don't know. It's just...all going to end."

They didn't agree on how. All agreed, the end was nigh, and started making plans.

I sat on the back doorstep, hands around my mug of tea, when Beth came back from checking next door again. His partner was flying home so they could be together when whatever happened did. The End of Days, for all their panic, but I struggled to believe it was that.

"Why aren't they trying to do something?" I asked.

She sat down beside me. "I think they're adjusting. Have you ever met a person whose family and friends have seen they're going to die? They drift away from them. They cut them out. They're used to looking to the future for solace and they can't find it. They've stopped looking. It must be terrifying."

Kat turned up two days later, fighting through a street party to get to our gate. There were puff pastry and crisp crumbs on the trestle tables. They played their favourite songs on loop, very, very loudly and I took to wearing headphones in the house so I didn't hear her knock.

"I'm sorry," she said.

I thought I wouldn't forgive her but Beth invited her in and gave her tea. After half an hour, we might have been sixteen again, sitting on the carpet with our pick-and-mix.

"So, how's it going to end?" I asked.

Beth kicked me in the shin. "Don't be so insensitive."

"They could just not look," I hissed.

"No, no. It's fine. It changes and it's all a bit of a blur anyway. You know..." but we didn't so she stopped.

"What I don't understand is how you never saw this coming before." I picked my way through a plate of custard creams, separating each into three pieces.

"I don't know."

The future changed, according to the actions taken by the people reacting to it. So, I supposed, someone, somewhere, did something to shift the paths of everyone in the world. Imagine having that kind of power.

Beth glared at me from where she sat on the settee, with one arm around Kat's shoulders. Kat was my friend, she was telling me without words.

I took Kat's hand, as people do on TV. "We'll get through this," I told her. "It always feels like the end of the world, but it never is. We just have to stay together and keep on going. One day at a time. We just have to...." I was going to say believe in the future, but she never had to. She always saw it. She'd forgotten how to hope.

She sniffed and gulped and looked to me. "How do you know?"

I smiled. "I've seen it all before."

I told her all the ways the world has ended and about the people I'd seen, walking through the ruins, living through the end. We would be them, I said. I told her how they looked when they woke one day, took a deep breath, and started to see the future again.

I hoped it helped her as much as it helped me.

The Skulk

J.M. Phillippe

J.M. Phillippe has lived in the deserts of California and the mad rush of New York City before finding her destiny in Tacoma, Washington. She worked as a freelance journalist before earning a masters' degree in social work and becoming a therapist. J.M. Phillippe is the author of the Book Excellence Award winning indie novel, The Christmas Spirit: a paranormal holiday adventure.

Devlyn Regan followed the trail past the fields of amaranth, the maroon stalks stretching as tall as him and waving gently in the morning breeze, and past the herb garden ringed by the golden-yellow blooms of the helichrysum, and toward the wood and metal coop. There, the paw prints danced around the edges of the wire that kept the pearl quails in and their predators out. Devlyn frowned.

Tending to the small birds had been his primary task since coming to the farm, their owner Sael having ordered him to feed and protect them. Their iridescent feathers in pale pinks and creamy whites ruffled at Devlyn's approach, and they hopped around their coop with irritated chirps and low whistles that sounded like water trickling over rocks. Devlyn checked the latch of the gate and found it secure. He examined the small house the birds nested in overnight, with a wooden ramp giving them easy access, and saw nothing amiss. He circled around, hands feeling out corners and edges of the pen and toes tapping the ground for soft spots that could be burrows under the fence, and found nothing. Everything seemed secure.

Except that the paw prints traced Devlyn's same path around the coop, yesterday's rain making soft molds of each one. A single creature, as far as Devlyn could tell. A curious creature. A dangerous creature.

Devlyn followed the prints back to the edge of the farm where they disappeared into the woods beyond. He should tell Sael, he thought, but the idea sat acidic in his stomach. There really wasn't anything to tell, was there? The quails seemed well and Sael was always so busy making salves and solutions, it would be a shame to disturb her work. Not to mention, scary. He spoke to her only when spoken to and kept as much distance as seemed appropriate for her servant.

Devlyn walked back toward the coop and around it, walking over the prints, obscuring them under his own. There was nothing left to report on after that. He briefly went inside the pen, carefully closing the gate behind him, and tossed seed and dried fruit around the yard which the quails pursued with excited hops. Then, he closed the gate securely again before walking back toward the house.

The surprisingly large home made of grey stone and sun-bleached wood loomed in front of him no less ominously than the day almost a moon ago when he was pushed toward it by his harried father. His father had not been a cruel man, just a poor one, and had been struggling to keep Devlyn and his younger siblings fed. And so, Devlyn was brought to Sael. Devlyn remembered being filled with dread as he walked up to the house, a scroll held tightly in his hand. He was one of only two people in his home who could even read it, his father being the other and the weaker reader. The scroll was from the Queen herself and dictated that Devlyn was the help Sael had requested.

Sael Eldrida, The Queen's Apothecary. She was both older and younger than Devlyn had expected, her silver hair always bound up in braids that circled the top of her head like a crown while her strong frame and thick arms and legs suggested a youthfulness that didn't seem to match. Devlyn had been expecting someone frail and bent, and was shocked at the energy, speed, and size of the Apothecary. She had looked Devlyn over that day with sharp green eyes, taking in the lankiness of his adolescent frame, the shabbiness of his loose-hanging clothes, the way his burnt-orange hair flopped pathetically to one side, and exhaled slowly.

"Very well," she had said, and immediately put him to work. She woke him each day just as the rays of sunlight started to break up the darkness of night, and she sent him to bed just as that same darkness crept back over the edge of the forest that surrounded the farm. She barked orders at him in short bursts: "fetch that bucket," "grind those seeds," "chop those herbs."

But, the pearl quails were his primary concern, Sael had told him. He'd never seen birds like them before, both familiar in shape and activity and foreign in color and song. They were a very rare breed, Sael told him, worth more than jewels. She didn't say why, and Devlyn didn't dare to press her for more information. In fact, he was unwilling to be in her presence more than necessary—he never forgot that she was a witch.

Still, he squared his shoulders as he pushed past the heavy wooden door of the house. Sael stood under a canopy of hanging herbs, a cacophony of scents filling the air around her—earthly and flowery, sharp and soft, medicinal and flavorful. Devlyn breathed it in with his usual enthusiasm, something about the mixture familiar to him even on his first day in the house, though he never could quite place it. Sael had his back to him as she carefully clipped bits off a bundle of herbs in her hands into a wooden bowl.

"How are the quails?" she asked, not turning to look at him.

"The birds are well. Still no eggs," he reported, fighting a shaking in his voice.

It had been the same every day for almost a moon and it felt like a personal failing that the birds he tended so carefully didn't produce.

But Sael just nodded.

"You will let me know the moment you see any," she said, glancing only briefly toward him as she gathered up her bowl and one other bundle of herbs that Devlyn couldn't quite recognize yet in their dried form, and moved toward the side of the house where both her chambers and workshop were. She entered her workshop, the metal-lined door thudding closed behind her. Devlyn breathed out the tension he'd been holding and went about his chores: adding logs to the fire always kept burning, sweeping up stray herbs from the floor, and taking buckets to fill at the well out front.

That evening, Devlyn checked the coop carefully and was relieved that there were no new tracks around it. In fact, the birds came running toward Devlyn and his basket of fruit and seed with something like friendliness, and he smiled as he entered the little house, back bent low. He methodically searched every nest as the birds ate, but no eggs had appeared during the day. Devlyn shrugged off his disappointment and patted the head of a nearby hen as though to reassure her he wasn't mad at her lack of eggs. She wriggled away from his touch, but did not peck him, which made him grin.

The next morning came on damp and cold, and Devlyn pulled on a thick black cloak before heading out toward the coop still bleary-eyed and in a mood made sour by the weather. The dampness had made new mud, and in the new mud were new prints at the edges of the fence. Devlyn's eyes quickly scanned the ground, the coop, the fence, and the few birds who had ventured from the warmth of their little house at the sound of his approach, looking for further signs of danger.

There! One perfect paw print, just inside the gate. One indented pad, four pointed toes, and four deep holes made by four sharp claws.

Devlyn rushed inside the gate as quickly as possible, counting the quails and searching out any sign of injury or abduction. The birds puffed and scattered, but they were all there, and each nest still empty of eggs. Devlyn searched the perimeter of the coop, pulling at the wire fencing, pushing against the wooden beams, looking for any possible way that any creature could get in or out. Then he went back to that single perfect paw print and stared. The gate was a snug fit, no gap along any edge, and the wires of the fence were shaped into holes too small to fit a paw through. It didn't make any sense, and a dark fear rose up in Devlyn. What if the pearl quails had been producing eggs? And what if this creature had been coming in every night to steal them?

But how? There was no way in, and no way out, save for the latch on the gate, too high and complex for anything that didn't have thumbs and human-height to manage. And yet, there was a paw print inside, and nests still empty, and the connection of the two took hold of Devlyn's imagination.

He should tell Sael. But, he didn't know what to tell her. His theory made no sense, and he feared that she would see his admittance as a failure to keep the pearl quails safe. Could he risk the witch's wrath? Better to solve it on his own, and since the birds themselves remained unharmed, all that he would be admitting was that the eggs might be stolen. *Might.* He still could not be sure. Devlyn went nervously back to the large stone house, pulling his cloak tighter about himself with worry.

Sael took the news of no eggs with her usual silent acceptance, and Devlyn declined to tell her anything else, convinced her silence meant he'd made the right choice. Instead, his thoughts circled the mystery, trying to work out possibilities. What could be making the paw prints? Why would it steal eggs and not hens? And what could Devlyn possibly do to stop it?

When all his questions were exhausted, Devlyn started working out a plan instead.

After Sael sent him to bed at dusk, Devlyn didn't change into night clothes and curl up under his thick quilts as he usually did. Instead, he waited until he could hear Sael retire, until there was no sound in the house at all. He opened his door slowly against the creek in the hinge, and waited to be sure Sael did not stir before moving as silently through the house as he could. He carefully lifted the large beam that secured the front door at night, and then he crept outside. He ducked behind shrubs at the edge of the house, and peered through the darkness toward the coop. The moon was not full above him, but fat and round enough to gleam against the metal wire and damp ground.

Devlyn kept as still as he could as the moments stretched on, his legs cramping beneath him. The light of the moon shifted as it continued its journey across the sky, and still Devlyn crouched, feet numb, hands stiff.

Finally, a movement at the edge of the amaranth field caught Devlyn's eye, and he forced himself statue-still. A shadow slunk forward, body low to the ground, pointed nose twitching as it revealed itself to be a fox, pale fur silvered by the moonlight, bright eyes gleaming. Devlyn watched as the fox crept forward and then dashed with surprising speed to the edge of the garden. It seemed completely unbothered by the yellow helichrysum that was supposed to deter pests of its kind. Devlyn could feel excitement pump blood back into his hands and feet. This had to be the same fox that had been visiting the coop at night, and now Devlyn would see how it was getting in and if it was in fact stealing the quail eggs.

The fox moved cautiously forward, and paused with perfect stillness halfway to the coop, its body parallel to where Devlyn was hiding.

Then the fox turned its head and stared directly at him. Its jaw fell open, and tongue lolled out, as though it were laughing at him. Fear and frustration coursed through Devlyn, and he jumped up, waving his hands. The fox jumped back, but didn't run away. Devlyn moved toward it, hands up to make himself bigger, and the fox pranced to the side, not the least bit afraid. Devlyn dashed forward. The fox dashed back. Devlyn lunged suddenly to the side, and the fox leapt the other direction, head down and front paws splayed out, playful.

"You won't get the eggs!" Devlyn shouted. "Argg! Get away!"

The fox stood up tall, nose in the air, sniffing, and still unafraid. Devlyn ran toward it and, at the last moment, the fox dashed to the side. Devlyn chased it past the garden and lost sight of it as it disappeared among the rows of maroon amaranth. Shaking, Devlyn bent over, hands on his knees, and breathed deeply. He'd never seen a fox that didn't run at the sight of a human. The ones on the edge of his father's farm were skittish things, easily spooked. This one was not only unafraid, it seemed to be playing with him. He shook his head, a chill seeping through his clothes and raising bumps on his skin. He shook off his fear and headed back to the coop with new weariness.

His eyes couldn't help but look inside the edges of the pen. Three more paw prints, creating a perfect triangle just below the ramp outside the quail's house, greeted him. No creature, not even one with three legs, could make such a design. Each paw print looked deliberate, perfectly pressed into the mud. Devlyn rubbed his hands over his eyes and looked again, and again the prints were there, an unnatural arrangement. Devlyn didn't bother going into the gate, counting the quails, or searching for eggs. It was too much. He felt defeated.

Instead, he went to wake Sael. What good was living with a witch if you couldn't take supernatural things to her? Even if he was afraid of what she might say or do to him, he knew that what he was dealing with was beyond his skill to manage. Head hanging and damp hair sticking to his forehead, he made his way back to the house and slipped inside. He walked slowly to Sael's chamber door, opposite her workshop, and took a deep breath. Then, he knocked.

Sael rose easily and came to her door shortly after Devlyn's timid knock.

"Yes?" Her voice was calm and unreadable.

"It's the quails," Devlyn blurted out. Sael stared at him for a long moment over the light of the lantern in her hand, and then nodded. She asked no questions but followed as he led her through the house, outside, and to the coop.

"There was a fox, and I chased it, and when I came back...." His voice cracked slightly as he spoke and he pointed helplessly at the paw prints glowing under the light of the moon. Then he looked back up at Sael, full of apprehension about what the witch might do.

Sael began to laugh. It was a hearty, full-bellied laugh that shook her shoulders and the long braid of her silver hair which flowed down her back. She laughed for a long time as Devlyn stood near her, his weariness slowly giving way to annoyance, and then anger.

"What could possibly be so funny?" he demanded in a tone he had never used with her before.

Sael wiped tears from her eyes and turned toward him.

"It's the skulk," she said. "They're playing with you."

Devlyn shook his head. "The foxes are taking the eggs! They have to be! There haven't been any, and I don't know how they've been getting in, but nothing else makes sense. And I don't understand what's so funny about it!"

Sael shook her head, not unkindly, and gestured for Devlyn to follow her. He did, mute in his anger and a little shocked that she hadn't yelled at him for his insubordination. She walked past the house and up a little hill on the other side. She led him to a spot at the base of an old oak tree, a hollow between its roots. Nestled inside was a small pile of flowers, each with two green stems ending in small bells of white petals clustered together in whorls.

"Moly," she said softly. "In exchange for pearl quail eggs."

Devlyn stared at the flowers in wonder, the light of the moon finding the white of the petals in a way that seemed impossible under the shadow of the tree. Moly, flower of the gods, said to be able to cure any ailment, even mortality itself.

"The foxes bring them?" he asked, unsure but starting to understand.

Sael nodded, satisfied with his conclusion.

"These are not your usual foxes, just as those are not usual quails. The skulk of these woods and I have an arrangement. They are clever, more clever than any other creature I know of, and so they can find the moly where others cannot, including myself. But of course, they want something in return. Pearl quail eggs are quite delicious."

"I was never going to find any eggs," Devlyn realized, almost sadly. Sael laid a gentle hand on his shoulder.

"Sometimes they will leave one or two behind," she said, her eyes glinting. "Next time they do, I'll let you keep one." She bent then and gathered up the flowers, making a basket in the folds of her robe. "Chin up, young one. They wouldn't play with you if they didn't like you. There's hope for you to become an apothecary yet."

"Me?" Devlyn's eyes went round like the moon above them. "No, I'm just supposed to help you, because the Queen said. And my family couldn't afford to keep me, and I'm not strong enough to work the fields, and so they sent me away...." His voice cracked at the last word. Sael smiled, and there was a sadness and sweetness in it he had never seen in her before.

"My dear boy, you weren't sent away. You were chosen." She watched his face as he took in the news, and he wasn't sure what she was reading, but she seemed satisfied enough to nod. "I wasn't completely sure—but if the skulk are playing with you, then they'll work with you. Yes, you are exactly who I hoped you'd be." She turned then and headed back to the house. "Don't dawdle," she barked over her shoulder in a tone that made Devlyn jump and run after her. But it didn't feel the same as before, a mean witch yelling at her servant. Because, Devlyn realized, he wasn't her servant, but her apprentice.

Her apprentice. But how?

A memory drifted to mind then. There had been a visitor to his parents' farm, hadn't there, when he was young? A cloaked figure that stood and watched him at his play. He hadn't remembered much of the visit, except that the smell coming off the figure was earthy and flowery, like an entire garden wafting toward him.

Or, like the hanging herbs that crowded the inside of Sael's house. Devlyn grinned, finally recognizing why the house smelled so familiar.

Chosen! It had to have happened then, when he was still small. Maybe that was why his parents allowed him to learn to read. Maybe that was why he was allowed time with his scrolls instead of in the fields.

Devlyn scurried along the path, following that same scent from his childhood back toward the house that now looked less ominous somehow, less large.

He paused before following his mentor into his home, turning to look back, his eyes searching and finding shadows in the garden, shadows in the field, and shadows near the coop, all with glinting eyes. The skulk.

Devlyn grinned and went inside.

After the Storm

A.M. Faller

Ally Faller is a recent graduate from the
University of Colorado Boulder with
dual degrees in Creative Technology
and Design and English, Creative
Writing. When she's not busy plotting
terrible situations to put her characters
in, you can find Ally outside running,
mountain biking, or skiing.

The sand was blowing again. It formed a cloud of stinging needles that whipped through the wind, threatening to scour the skin from her bones as it had the vegetation from the sandstone dunes. Aza wrapped her canvas scarf tighter around her face, trying not to breathe too deeply. The fine particles would work their way into the lining of her lungs soon enough, reducing her capacity to inhale and stealing years of her life, but she'd been lucky so far on the journey—she'd found abandoned but functional BioShields before the last two storms. This time, it didn't seem she'd be so fortunate. When the wind started to change and the moisture was sucked out of the air, there was nothing before her but the monotonous waves of pale stone trapped in their eternal swells and rolls and the wide, yellow expanse of the sky.

Aza wasn't willing to push the glider any faster—her sail already strained and snapped in the wind despite being nearly completely furled. She scanned the horizon again, chest tightening, hoping for a glimpse of the life-saving green that might indicate an oasis outpost. Nothing but the white stone waves and crags of the Barren met her eyes. A glance over her shoulder confirmed her fears about the changing weather. The mass of the storm was little more than a hazy red outline on the horizon, but she knew that it would be upon her by the time the hour was out. Aza gave the sail a bit more slack, flying across the stone so quickly the little craft threatened to shake to bits. This wasn't how she imagined her first posting—rattling into the oasis half-dead, flayed by sandstorms, in a glider that was little more than a child's toy. And alone. That part was the worst. She shouldn't be alone. No one traveled alone across the great expanse, the Barren, unless they were feral, but the Council of Seven simply didn't have anyone to send with her at the time, and the Lostara Oasis was about to run out of water. Resources were stretched thin, she knew. Half a dozen wells had gone dry in the last three cycles, and the council was forced to send out trainees to evacuate the citizens of the unlucky oases. Still, she'd been the only Dowser sent without an escort.

The situation was strained in the capital, but here, facing the waves of white stone and the sun-swallowing blood red mass behind her, far from the towering Biowalls and lush gardens that protected the Council of Seven and Asoria City, she couldn't suppress her rising anger. They shouldn't have made her pour her energy into years of training if they were going to send her out to the desert and her death.

She gave her head a vicious shake, trimming the sails again and forcing more speed from the glider. It didn't do any good to linger over the decisions of the Council. They had far more information than she did, and they wouldn't have given her the grave responsibility of relocating the Lostara Oasis if they weren't confident in her abilities. She shouldn't doubt the Council's decision, and she certainly didn't want to prove them wrong. They'd taken a risk on her, and she wanted to prove that she was worth it—that the circumstances of her birth weren't going to define her.

Aza glanced back again. The storm was close enough now that she could see the swirls of differently colored sand and dust, scoured from the surface of the Barren. It was beautiful, the black, gold, and red streams that rolled through the wave of sand, but she knew it would kill her in moments if she were caught in the open. Aza scowled, debating internally. It was forbidden to use her power exclusively for her own gain, but surely an exception would be made if it permitted her to successfully complete her journey and lead the people of the Lostara Oasis to a new well-site. She hesitated, eyes still fixed on the swirling mass that swallowed the landscape. A violent flare of lightning arcing through the storm made up her mind, and she stretched her power forward into the dead earth ahead of her. She Dowsed in vain for a moment, despair blooming every second that she detected nothing except emptiness, but a glimmer caught her attention. Aza latched onto the miniscule spark of life, swinging the rudder of her glider to angle further south, off of her course and towards a massive fissure in the rolling white stone.

She dropped the magnetic anchor of the glider at the edge of the crevice, frantically untying knots and untangling lines to gather the sail cloth in her arms. Aza shoved the cloth into the metal-lined chest that ran along the edge of the glider as the first few stinging bits of sand hit her exposed arms. They felt like nothing more than a tingle, but a single crimson drop of blood pattered onto the deck, the laceration so fine it was invisible. She hissed, pulling her pack over her shoulder and leaping from the deck. Landing lightly on her toes, Aza ran towards the edge of the cravace. She peered over the edge for a moment, staring tentatively into the black depths beneath her. If there was a water source and BioShield down there, she couldn't see it. Then again, this is what she had trained for all of those years. She was a Dowser—she didn't need to see water to be certain of its presence. Hissing with pain as the sting of the sand increased, Aza took a few steps back, casting a MagLine behind her. It fixed on the stone with a gentle click, and, with a firm test tug, she planted her feet on the edge of the fissure, took the cable in her hands, and began the descent. Aza had always been more athletic than the other, oasis- or capital-born Dowsers. It had set her apart, easy fodder for snide, cruel comments, and she'd quickly learned to wear long, excessively loose clothing to disguise her naturally muscular form. As she repelled into the crevice, though, the wind growing from a whistle to a scream above her, she was grateful for both her "uncultured" strength and the tight, non-regulation clothing she'd slipped into her pack for the journey.

Aza had guided her craft well—her Dowsing had always been accurate—and only had to swing a few feet to land on the ledge from which the sparkle of life emanated. Between the shadows of the crevice and the rapidly darkening sky, it took a moment of fumbling in the gloom to find the moss film on the cliff wall. Her blindly groping hands sunk into the spongy material, fingers pushing depressions into the dense, moist pad. She was surprised at how fresh the BioShield felt—she'd expected it to be dried out, struggling to sap the last few drops of remaining moisture from the parched air, but it was nearly as thick and lush as if it was new grown. By the time she'd felt her way to the edge of the pad and peeled it away from the cliff wall, shards of sand were beginning to hiss down the sides of the crevice.

It wasn't a large BioShield, only about a foot and a half wide and five or so feet tall. She had to duck slightly and turn sideways to squeeze through the crack it exposed, spilling out into an open space and pulling the Shield tight against the wall behind her. It was perfectly dark and damp, the air heavy with the scent of rotting vegetation, but the hiss of the sand and scream of the wind was swallowed by the mossy Shield. Aza shivered slightly, suddenly missing the searing heat of the double suns. She pulled the light stick from her pack, shaking it violently. It flickered, but slowly grew to a blue-green glow that illuminated a bit of the space around her.

She was in a chamber, half the natural, rounded corners of the sandstone and half showing the distinctive pattern of rectangular chisel marks from human hands. It wasn't a large space, but there were a few blankets folded neatly in one corner and a stout chest tucked in the other. Rudimentary shelving had been hacked into the southernmost wall. She opened the chest, expecting the usual array of Asoria City certified and Dowser distributed dried goods stacked in neat piles. It took her a moment to process the neatly stacked items. There were piles of goods, but in small quartz boxes and tightly stitched and oiled furs rather than the transparent algal layer of capital city packaging. It had been more than a decade since the capital had used any sort of animal products, and this BioShield certainly wasn't that old. More than that, she'd memorized the maps of every shelter between the capital city and Lostara Oasis, and this one, as small as it was, wasn't marked. She frowned slightly, gazing around again at the chisel marks in the stone walls. There was no record of ferals ever making their own shelters—they were willing to steal and kill decent oasis citizens for mere drops of water. She couldn't think of another explanation, though. This shelter didn't grow out of the cliff face out of its own volition—someone built it, and the Council of Asoria didn't know it existed.

Her frown deepened, and she slipped her hand into her bag, folding back the false bottom to access a hidden pocket. Aza felt a wave of guilt as she pulled the bone knife carefully from the pouch. The capital had strict regulations against the possession of animal products, but, as her classmates never permitted her to forget, her parents weren't from the capital. Dowsers weren't permitted to carry weapons, either. They were intended to be Astoria's agents of peace, and she would have been severely chastised and likely placed in solitary confinement if she'd been found with the blade. Aza tried to follow the Council's many rules, tried to be as obedient, modest and self-sacrificing as a good citizen should be, but she couldn't bring herself to get rid of the last traces of her family. The knife, a charm, and a few blurry memories of raised voices, screaming wind, and golden sand were all she had left. She'd been little more than an infant when she'd been abandoned just outside of the city walls, wrapped tightly in a ragged blanket just before the worst sandstorm in recorded history swept in, scraping the land clean of every living thing that wasn't behind a BioShield. Her teachers in the academy, guardians, and advisors throughout her life reminded her that she was lucky. Lucky her feral parents saw the wisdom of giving her a chance at life in the capital, lucky the patrol had found her and brought her within the city walls, and, most of all, lucky she was the first and only of *her kind* to be born with a drop of the Dowsing power.

As she sat and listened to the wind scream outside, shivering slightly in the damp chill of the crack, she didn't feel particularly lucky. Aza placed a tentative hand on the weave of the BioShield. It fluttered like a frightened heartbeat but held firm against the blades of sand she knew pummeled it from the other side. Aza allowed her light stick to flicker out, leaned her head back against the cold wall of the shelter, and calmed her breathing. She couldn't guess how long the storm would be raging outside—from what she'd seen on the glider, it had looked massive. A storm of that size should have been predictable, should have been something the Council warned her of. But then again, she should have been traveling to her first assignment with a full support team, equipt with portable BioShields and advanced storm prediction. Nothing about this situation was typical for the launch of a new Dowser, and as much as she tried to explain it away, the pit of insecurity rolling in her gut told her that the Council wouldn't have been so unconcerned if she'd been born in the capital, or even one of the oases. She returned her focus to slowing her heartbeat to near stasis. As calm descended upon her, a more positive thought drifted into her mind. Maybe they'd sent her because they knew she was the only one that could find a way to survive such a journey unsupported and lead the people of Lostara Oasis to safety before their water ran out completely. After all, surviving unsupported in the Barren was what ferals excelled at, and after spending years defending oases and the capital from the ferals' scattered incursions, the Council should know that better than anyone. She smiled slightly before letting her mind slide away completely.

The silence brought Aza out of her trance. She placed a tentative hand on the BioShield, which hung damp and still once more. The wind had slipped back to its normal murmur rather than the scream of the storm. A few more moments of careful listening confirmed that the hiss of sand had vanished. She slipped through the BioShield, pulling her pack over her shoulder and stepping onto the sand-scoured ledge. Her cable hung, drifting lazily a few feet away, and she used the short ledge to run a few paces before throwing herself into the air. Her hands caught the cable, but she still slid a few feet, burning her palms. Mag cables, being made to retract smoothly, weren't pleasant to climb, but she eventually threw an exhausted arm over the edge of the ravine and scrambled over the sandstone lip. Aza jogged to her glider, relieved the storm was intense but not particularly long. The craft seemed mostly unharmed, and after a few moments of digging, she cleared the lee-ward side of the sand drifts that had formed. A few grains of sand had found their way through the sealed sail box, but the thick cloth was whole. After a bit of cloth-shaking and line-tying, the craft was skimming along again, hurtling shakily towards the Lostara Oasis.

Aza glanced up from her chart, scanning the horizon. She saw the towering red cliffs that sheltered the oasis from the worst of the storms and the deep crack in the rock through which the community was nestled, but the warding houses marked on her map were missing. There should have been a pair of BioShelters squatting at the base of the cliff, waiting to welcome travelers and keeping watch for storms or wandering bands of ferals. She was sure that this was the right canyon—she was a good navigator, and the surrounding landmarks were exactly as had been described to her. For a moment, she thought that the shelters had perhaps been buried under sand drifts from the most recent storm. But no, as she pulled her craft closer to the cliff, she could see where they should have stood, moored to the soft stone by a series of carved eyelets. They were not buried—they were simply gone. Perhaps they'd already been packed up in preparation for the impending move. Aza tried to shrug off the missing watch shelters as she nosed her craft into the narrow canyon, but a flame of nervousness lit in her stomach and refused to be stifled.

She drifted slowly around the bends in the canyon, carefully piloting around jutting overhangs and sudden turns. The sun was nearing the horizon when she finally made her way around the last outcropping of rock, spilling out of the rift in the cliff walls and into the small valley that sheltered the Lostara Oasis.

Aza gazed out at the expanse of empty sand stretching in front of her, littered with the skeletons of a few buildings before ending in another sheer cliff face. Nothing grew, nothing moved. Even the eternal wind didn't sigh in this silent nook that should have been teeming with life. She leapt from her glider, not bothering to drop anchor, and strode towards the ruins that should have been a sanctuary. A few wooden frameworks corroded to delicate spires by the sand and wind still stood, but the elaborate water catchment system, the dozens of homes and BioShields, the gardens and animals that should have been nestled in the valley were gone—long gone, if the height of the sand dune were any indication. Aza kicked a loose stone violently, letting out a shout of frustration and agony that bounced off the cliff walls before echoing into the uncaring sky.

"What's this about, now?" said a grating voice from behind her. She whirled, startled to see a weathered man dressed in layers of beige canvas standing at the mouth of the canyon, next to her glider. He held a crude bow in his hands, arrow knocked but held loosely, pointed at the ground.

"Step away from the glider, sir," Aza said, striding towards him. By the sun beaten look of his face, the makeshift weapons, and the rags of canvas sailcloth, he must be a feral, hoping to scavenge what little remained of the Lostara Oasis. The man spit on the sand, a supreme insult from someone who ought to treasure moisture.

"You talk Capital," he said. He looked at her for a moment, head cocked, before snapping up the bow, drawing, and firing in a single fluid motion. Aza squaked, darting left and throwing herself into a graceless roll. She came to her feet in a low crouch. She was eyeing the distance to the glider, wondering if she could make a dash for the deck, where her pack and knife sat, when another voice spoke from behind her.

"Don't move too Capital, though, do you, darling? Those oafs don't know their rump from their cap. What're you doing out here?"

Aza slid a few steps backwards, pivoting so she could see both of the ferals. A woman stood to her right, wrinkled face topped by a cloud of grey hair. Despite her apparent age and the long staff she held, she stood perfectly still and erect. Aza immediately got the feeling that the staff was a weapon, not a crutch, and woe upon any fool that didn't draw the same conclusion. She considered the couple for a moment. The man's head was cocked, bow lowered once more, and he looked at her curiously. The woman's eyes, shockingly blue, were surrounded by a net of crow's feet and smile lines. Aza hesitated momentarily.

"I appear to have been sent to die," said Aza, unable to keep either the bitter bite or the choke of tears from her voice. The woman clucked sympathetically, but the man gave a braying laugh which turned to a hacking cough.

"Well, that makes all of us, child," he said, recovering himself. "Strange that the Council is chucking younglings out to the Barren, now though. What'd you do? Spirituality? Asked questions? Refused to sleep with the wrong Councilor?" The woman gave the man a sharp look, but her eyes swung to Aza, obviously waiting for her answer. Aza stood still for a moment before exhaling sharply, glaring at the sky.

"I existed, I guess. I wasn't born in the capital, and they took offense."

"Born in an oasis?" said the woman.

Aza shook her head. "Feral. My parents left me at the gates."

Both the man and the woman frowned at the word, and Aza shrugged apologetically.

"Unassociated or nomadic is better. But call us what you will, we don't leave our babes, and the capital certainly doesn't take them in. Not exactly known for their affection, those arrogant thieves. How'd you end up here in a glider instead of at a mining camp?" The woman rubbed her staff between her hands, letting it twist a divot in the sand.

Aza eyed them hesitantly. Beyond their initial ferocity, they didn't seem particularly threatening. Besides, she desperately needed help—she'd been relying on the oasis to restock on food and water before leading the people to a new water source, and there was no way she'd survive the trip back to the capital on what she had. Not that she wanted to return to Astoria. She looked at the strip of yellow sky that peeped through the canyon's walls, scanning the sheer cliffs and glancing again at the abandoned ruin that should have been her oasis. Finally, she met first the man's suspicious brown eyes and the woman's keen blue gaze.

"I have certain skills that were in short supply. Not short enough, I guess, for them to get over their prejudice."

The man's gaze became speculative. "Well," he said slowly, finally un-nocking the arrow, "my Vik can weave as good of a BioShield as you'll see outside the capital, so we're doing quite well. But if there's something else you can offer..."

Aza gave him a bitter smile. "I can Dowse." The man smiled in return, displaying even, shockingly white teeth, and she heard the woman's short intake of breath.

"You'd be welcome to join us, but you are sure you don't want to go to a different oasis? Back to the capital? It isn't a comfortable life out here," the woman said.

Aza shook her head. "It wasn't comfortable there, either. I'd rather be with people who wouldn't send me into the Barren to die."

The woman smiled as well, reaching out to offer a hand. "Well, then. Perhaps you'd like to meet the rest of our little family group."

Shaking her hand, Aza let her surprise show on her face. The woman chuckled.

"They might call us feral, but we get along with each other well enough. You didn't think that everyone was pleased with the Council's rules, did you?"

"I didn't think there was another option," Aza said, following the woman back towards the crack in the cliff where a second, equally rickety glider sat moored behind her own.

The woman laughed. "Oh, child," she said, "come. Come see the other option. It isn't the luxury you can find in the capital, but I have a feeling you'll like it far better."

Home

Robin Kirk

Robin Kirk is the author of The Bond and The Hive Queen, books one and two in a fantasy trilogy. The Mother's Wheel completes the series and will be published in 2022. Her short stories and poems have appeared in speculative fiction and other publications. Kirk has published three nonfiction books on human rights in Latin America as well as essays, articles, short stories, and opeds. She teaches human rights at Duke University.

A warning buzz wakes her. She'd been dreaming. She struggles to remember. Clouds? Falling? Whatever it was, her heart still races.

The buzz means that some sort of craft has locked onto the docking platform. The platform's a perk she gets for serving as stations commander. In the dock are two berths, one for the transport she uses to go between the five stations orbiting Venus and one for visitors.

She wonders: *could this be him?*

With a bump, the craft's nose reaches the lock. She hears a thunk as the clamps, well, clamp. The cradle in the visitor berth creaks as the craft settles.

Her son's racing skiff? She listens harder.

What she wants to hear is this: the scrape of his hatch. It's never been quite right since...well, since the accident several months ago. Minor in the end. It could have been worse. So much worse. What's important is that the seal is still good. The seal held. And the safety protocols, well. They did what they were supposed to do.

Protocols over the brain and reaction time of a young man. He always wanted to be a pilot despite his recklessness. Maybe because of it? What combination of attention to detail and recklessness makes a good pilot?

His father was too reckless. But their boy...Did the accident teach him a lesson? Is he more cautious now? Does he think two, no three steps ahead? Five? Eighteen?

The hatch scrapes.

Good. Her boy.

"Drop three degrees," she says out loud. "No, five. Drop five degrees." Her son likes it a little frosty.

The thermostat responds with a tickle of cold air. Her bedroom flashes briefly with the green light confirming an arrival. The system recognizes the craft and authorizes airlock entry.

She doesn't turn on the reading light. She doesn't get up.

A thrum of footfalls approaches the airlock. He's so like his father. A heavy walker and graceless off the basketball court and out of the cockpit. Yet with a ball in his hands, a throttle, he's liquid, like quicksilver. He can leap a solid two feet into the air, do a 180, a 360, and arc the ball into the net. He can spin his racing skiff and blast it out at a 90-degree angle.

Sometimes, she thinks her boy is all arcs and angles. Hard to hold on to, always has been.

So she listens.

What would it be like to play ball on Terra now, he mused the last time he visited. His ball-handling skills are awesome, he self-reports, but he'd have to work hard to counter the toll of artificial gravity: build better muscle tone, more stamina. Reasonably, he told her he'd have to work hard on bone density, the bane of off-worlders.

Her boy: a planner. His shoes would feel like lead, not neoprene, he'd remarked. He'd palm that ball intending to launch it into a spinning arc, then see it sink heavy and unyielding as a tank of air.

He'd get there, she told him. He's a hard worker. He'd rise.

With a whoosh, the airlock opens. A spritz of decontaminant—measures still in place even though the last recorded infection was months ago—is like the slip of a blanket off the bed. The inner door slides open, then closes and seals with a soft thwack.

But does he go to the guest room? Of course not. He's like his racing skiff, always in need of fuel. The refrigerator door opens. A plate and a knife slap against the countertop. She thinks she hears the splurge of mayo though it's probably her imagination. He's always been one for intense flavors: stone-ground mustard, wasabi, bhut jolokia sauce, gochujang.

She'd tucked bottles of beer on the lower shelf just in case he stopped by, like gold coin to be discovered in one of his online quests. Does he see them? Still, she doesn't get up. There's something sacred about these unannounced visits, these kitchen raids. It's like he's reaching out to her through space: close but not too close. He still needs her. She doesn't want to ruin it with her presence, her questions, her concern.

She savors the sounds like he must savor what he's eating.

She hears the decisive tap of a beer bottle against the counter, the ting of a dislodged cap. A Martian Pilsener, expensive, but worth it. The beer, the food: they draw him if only for a night.

He's tuned the jabber of his com low. As always, he doesn't sit - she hears no scrape of the stool, no settling of his body. His hunger is everything and must be quelled. Then the plate goes into the sink, a knife clattering. In 18 years, never once has a plate ever made it all the way into the dishwasher. The dishwasher might as well be in another galaxy.

She doesn't mind. In the morning, while he's still asleep, she'll test what she heard against the evidence: what's still on the plate, what's missing from the refrigerator, the empty bottle of Pilsener.

She hears his heavy tread again, to the toilet for a decisive piss: door open, luxurious, prolonged. A swipe of the toothbrush off the rack, a sizzle of water from the faucet. He's a man now, she reminds herself, not a child who needs to be reminded to be thorough.

Yet. He still comes.

Worry is an itch she can't satisfy. Be careful when you shuttle between stations. Be careful when you make that turn in your race. Make sure, above all, that you don't spiral into the acid clouds that still wreath the planet, that you don't come to grief on the super-heated plains.

That she doesn't come to grief on those plains. Again.

Still, she hears the com humming with voices. The broadcast could be Terra or Mars or one of her stations, pinned above the planet like miniature stars. The mattress crinkles as he sits. His now-empty boots thump to the floor. He groans softly as he lays back. She listens for the grumble as he shifts, asleep.

Her boy. *Home.*

Bluebell Song

JL George

JL George lives in Cardiff and writes weird and speculative fiction.

Old Woman Achan goes out to the woods before dawn and sits amid the undergrowth and fills her ears with the song of the bluebells. To a stranger it would look like a pleasure-jaunt, and an ill-advised one too, but Achan chooses her place carefully. She listens with intent. When she closes her eyes, she imagines she hears the bluebells move, craning their bright heads toward her. Of course, when she opens them again, nothing has changed. The flowers hang delicate as raindrops from their stems. Looking at them, Achan thinks a single touch might send them tumbling to the ground. Each petal curls back neatly from the mouth of the flower, leaving them open in endless song.

When her daughter Tiwan was young, she was careful to caution the girl against getting too close to the flowers. All parents did. There was a reason bluebells had once been thought to belong to the fair folk. To listen to their song was to succumb to a slow madness, drawn back to hear them again and again until you wasted away, wandering the woods like a wraith, neither sleeping nor eating, only listening. To fill your mouth with that music, though—to trap it and drink it down like nectar—was to be healed of sickness and injury and sorrow, to feel the blood thrum like sap in your veins, to shine. To enchant all around you as the bluebells did, and be loved and heard always.

That was a problem, of course. Who would wish to be as the bluebell to her loved ones? But in any case, the flowers did not sing for those who stopped up their ears, and so it was futile to try. The risk was too great. Nobody knew the woods better than Achan, but even she had only ever told her daughter, *Carry wax with you to stop up your ears. Tread carefully, and whatever you do, don't listen.*

But now she nestles amid the bluebells and lets their song fill her up until she feels her head will float from her shoulders; until she dreams she sees a golden door in the woods and the song is the shining thread that will lead her to it. It hums beneath her skin and warms her bones, the arthritic ache in her knuckles fading. Though it is dark, she feels warm as a cat in the sun. The warmth is deceptive, she knows, but it's hard to resist sinking into it, harder than getting out of a cosy bed on a winter's morning.

A small voice sounds near the edge of the wood. "Grandmother! Grandmother, come quickly! Mama's worse again."

The golden door fades from view, the warmth dissipating. Achan gathers up her skirts and picks her way through the bluebells, making for the treeline as briskly as her legs will carry her. Not as fast as they used to, that's for sure.

Sichen waits at the edge of the wood, tugging nervously at a tall fern. Achan takes his hand. "Did you bring wax with you? For your ears? We're close to the bluebells here."

The boy looks down guiltily. "I didn't think. I was scared."

Achan shakes her head. "Didn't your mother remind you?"

"She's busy looking after Mama." Sichen chews his lip. "I think she's scared, too."

* * *

Tiwan is coughing hard when they reach the house. She sleeps on the couch on the ground floor now, for she wheezes like an old woman when she climbs the stairs. The once-warm brown of her complexion is ashen, her strong arms wasted almost to the bone. She still wears the silver bracelet Mira, her wife, gave her on their wedding day, but it hangs off her skinny wrist as though she is a child again, playing dress-up with Achan's own wedding jewellery, parading around the house and calling, "Look, Mama, I'm the queen of the world!" At the time, Achan barely spared her a glance, a distracted smile. She didn't have the temperament to laugh and play along with a child's games, so she left all that to Twm—though if she had the time again, she'd try.

Time trickles away so fast when you're not paying attention, and Tiwan has little left. Achan has tried everything she knows. None of it has worked.

Mira fusses over the stove, heating water for sage tea. Her movements are more practised these days, but she's neither a healer nor a cook by nature. Her skills have always been in teaching, and the local children learn their letters far more slowly without her guidance. Learning to play the nurse has been hard on her: there are deep shadows beneath her eyes and her wispy yellow hair looks like it's seen neither brush nor water in weeks. Sichen goes to her and she squeezes him tight, his face buried against her side. "Tell me there's something else we can try," she says, looking at Achan with desperate eyes. "Tell me you've got something."

Silent, Achan goes to her daughter's bedside. Tiwan blinks up at her in surprise when Achan reaches for her hand. They clasp and hold on, neither as strong as she would wish to be.

"Nothing yet," she tells Mira.

Then she kisses Tiwan's forehead and returns to the forest.

* * *

Old Woman Achan goes out to the woods before dawn; and in the golden mid-morning and the heat of midday and at twilight; and some of the neighbours say they hear the door of her cottage opening even in the dead of night. Her grief has driven her to the bluebells, they whisper. Even her skill cannot save her daughter now, and, having given up hope, she seeks only escape.

It's not entirely a lie. She's always found it easier to entangle herself in the quiet life of plants. The closeness of people is noisier, more demanding, and she struggles to say the right words and make the right faces. But identifying a herb by the shape of its leaves, harvesting the right amount, mixing up a remedy—that's a different matter. Achan may not be able to charm people into friendship or make them laugh with witty remarks, but she can take pleasure in accomplishing a healing, in the silent interactions of leaf and flesh, sap and blood.

When Twm was alive, things were easier. They each had their own domains, she the forest and he the town. Without him, she feels half-in, half-out of both, unmoored and drifting.

She sits very still on the ground and listens well. A beetle crawls over her foot as though it is a tree root. A curious squirrel picks acorns from the dirt at the hem of her skirts. Achan does not move.

The bright door floats before her eyes, sketched in glowing lines of bluebellsong. She does not know what's on the other side— only that it is beautiful, and terrible. Her heart beats hard at the thought of seeing it, but the song gentles it again.

The song puts down roots in her, digs up long-buried childhood imaginings of treetrunk doors that lead to other worlds. Achan feels the living wood around and above her, the slow movement of sap and the unfurling of leaves. She sways with the breeze that moves the bluebells and rustles the canopy. She creeps through the earth with the roots of all vegetal things. The lines between what is Achan and what is the forest begin to blur.

She never quite reaches the door; but she gets a little closer every time. And when the song ends and she is surfeited with it, there is a faint hint of something left over. A silvery tone in the air, perhaps, the last echo of some unknown verse.

Then—then—Old Woman Achan recovers herself. With whatever small hard core of will she has left, she forces herself to turn from the golden door and to sink ever so gently back to earth. She plucks from the folds of her skirt a small glass vial and uncorks it, and the last note of the song fades from hearing. Achan breathes in deeply, burying her fingers in the grass to anchor herself before she can climb to her feet.

The vial is almost a third of the way full, now. Tiwan grows paler every day, her lucid moments less frequent. This morning she coughed up blood and Mira sent Sichen down to the river until lunchtime so he wouldn't hear her crying. Through the window, Achan watched him dawdling by the water, apart from the games and races of his friends, looking homeward, where once he'd been first into the water, his voice the loudest in the joyful din. A boy his age ought not to be so solitary, so drawn in on himself; but then a boy his age ought not to watch his mother fade like light in autumn.

Achan held Mira's hand while she cried, remembering how she'd held it on the day of the wedding, welcoming her to the family. Twm had still been alive then, his own brilliant smile the original of Tiwan's, father and daughter beaming side by side as he walked her to the altar. Now, Tiwan lies with her eyes closed in the sleep of pure exhaustion, no expression on her face at all.

* * *

Old Woman Achan goes out to the woods and she does not come home.

The evening darkens, and her daughter wakes briefly from fitful sleep to ask for her. Mira wipes her brow and gentles her, and then tells Sichen to stop his ears up with wax and go searching.

The boy's heart beats fast, made louder by the plugs in his ears, as he passes the treeline. He wants to hurry but finds himself creeping carefully through the trees, holding his breath when he sees the misty carpet of bluebells and the dark form crumpled in their midst.

His grandmother is not moving. Her eyes gaze sightlessly up at him, and the fingers of her right hand dig root-like into the soil. Clutched in her left is a glass vial, with something inside it that moves like oil and shines like the moon.

Sichan runs weeping home to his mothers, the vial held tight in his fist. When he shows it to Mira her breath hitches in her throat and she sends him from the room.

He listens hard at the door. For a moment golden light creeps through the crack beneath it and there is a sound like a heavy old door opening, and a snatch of strange music. And, for a moment, Sichan imagines he hears his grandmother's voice.

It fades as quickly as it came. When Mira calls him back inside, Tiwan is sitting up in bed, and for the first time in many weeks there is colour in her cheeks. The glass vial sits empty on the nightstand.

* * *

Old Woman Achan is buried at the edge of the woods. Tiwan has to sit down for most of the service, and when she stands she leans heavily on Mira, but day by day she grows stronger. At last she is well enough to roam the woods as her mother once did, picking herbs to treat the illnesses of neighbours and friends, pointing out the plants good to eat and the ones that are poison to her son, who shadows her so closely they seem almost one figure. People listen to her. She seems to speak with her mother's old authority now.

Mira begins to laugh again, and if there is something distant and dreamy in her eyes when she regards her wife, well, it looks like a happy dream. Sichan grows in confidence again, running around with the other children, no longer afraid something terrible will happen if he is away from home too long. If he still seems a little more eager than the others to return home to his mother at dusk, well, it's hardly a surprise after all he's been through. Things are good.

And if sometimes Tiwan leaves the house before dawn and returns with her skirts soaked to the knee—well, she always returns smiling. When Mira stirs in bed and asks her where she's been she only says, "There's nothing to worry about." When she speaks there is a silvery echo in the air, fading like the final note of a half-heard song.

Relapse

Phoenix Roberts

Phoenix lives and works on the East coast.
Among other things, she writes horror
fiction, but would like the reader to know
that she's very fun at parties, and hardly
ever cavorts with murderous shadowy
figures. Her poetry has previously
appeared in Paintbucket magazine.

It was small and unimportant and by her own estimation it was the greatest thing Katherine had ever done. It was a table, one foot wide and one-point-five feet long—or it would be as soon as she finished it. Big enough to eat at. At six months, she'd been working on it for five months and twenty-seven days longer than expected. In her opinion, the problem wasn't that she lacked commitment to the project. The problem was that she kept being distracted by something she saw, or thought she saw, out of the corner of her eye, and something she felt, or thought she felt, on the hairs of her skin.

On Sunday morning, the crows outside her window cawed her to waking and she yawned her way to the half-bathroom four feet from her floor mattress. Over the sound of piss hitting the bowl, she noticed that for the first time in a long, long time her panties were splattered red. She imagined herself God creating Adam when she strutted out and pointed her middle finger at the checklist taped to her front door. There were only three items left: *Screw, Sand,* and *Dye*. There was another list on the other side, the side pressed to the door, and that was the side that could choke. That was the side that officially did not matter anymore. She had her whole period back.

It struck her when she least expected it, the seeing and the feeling.

It snuck up on her just when she picked up her saw, reached out and softly encircled her wrist while she was sprawled out on the floor with her measuring tape. That particular Sunday, it flickered around the corners of her computer screen, grabbing her attention from a misspelled comment about sturdiness. For three hours, she compared the merits and drawbacks of two competing screw companies. She could have spent even more time. The carpentry forums had no rules about how long an interloper could mill around, parsing reviews. That was the great thing about making a table, as opposed to some other tasks. The minutes were free things, subject to her whims and her whims alone. There was nothing to add or subtract, nothing was wasted in wasting, and in no time at all four legs would hold up a surface she could put plates and bowls on.

What she saw, or what she thought she saw, was a mass of grey things, moving quickly in no direction. What she felt, or what she thought she felt, was a gentle pull.

Her pencil was too dull to write down the name of the screw company with the fewest angry reviews, so she sharpened it. The wood shavings succumbed to the pull, floated through the air and stuck to the wall of her apartment facing the street, where the storage closet was dug in. There was grey movement in the space between the door and the linoleum tiles underneath. She could have put an end to it right then and there, looked the contents of her storage closet dead in the face and escaped the nauseous uncertainty which had so far thwarted her nascent table. Instead, she closed her eyes shut as tight as she could, and when she opened them the only thing beneath that door was lint.

At the home goods store, she bought the right brand of screws and she splurged on a glossy red dye for the top of the table. On the bus ride back, she crinkled open her plastic bag of goodies and ran her index finger over the side of the dye can, her chest thrumming with excitement and pride that only faltered a little when she saw that she forgot to buy sandpaper. In the bag, she saw wisps of grey unfurling in the space where a sandpaper packet should have been, and then she blinked and they were gone.

In her building, Cherry was in the hallway. Katherine waved. Cherry paused to adjust her messenger bag and unclip her bike helmet.

"Did you know that the cause of most power outages in the U.S. is none other than the humble squirrel?" Cherry asked. Cherry liked collecting facts and bestowing them on others when she felt the moment was right. When the moment was right, her eyes got wide and glittery and the *Did you know* happened breathlessly, like she was about to burst from the pressure of a salacious secret. Katherine liked this. She also liked that Cherry never wore two of the same sock. That particular Sunday, it was one maroon and one teal. Looking at them made Katherine happy. She pictured Cherry in the morning, rooting around the drawer for a matching pair, throwing up her hands like *fuck it, there are more important things*. This was the other great thing about making a table, as opposed to some other projects. It challenged, but not so much that the intricacies of other people were impossible. Katherine thought that Cherry lived a very interesting life, meaning that the two of them probably had little in common.

"By the way," Cherry added, "You're looking better these days. Healthier. More life in the eyes." Katherine counted to three and sucked in a long breath. The space behind Cherry's head went grey. Although Katherine's fist sat perfectly still around the bag handle, its contents shifted, the weight leaning a little bit towards the front door of her apartment. She knew it was the pull.

"I did *not* know that about squirrels," she said, and to prove to herself and to Cherry that she was perfectly content with being described as *Healthy*, she walked into her apartment and baked a tray of chocolate chip cookies and she wrapped it in aluminum and brought it to Cherry's door. If she spat out the single chocolate chip that found its way to her mouth in the making, it didn't mean a thing.

The corner store sold everything. Everything likely included sandpaper. She hadn't been there in six months. She'd prefer not to go there for another six months at least, but that preference was more faint than her patience for another bus ride to the home goods store.

Outside there was a girl, or rather a woman, maybe a year younger than Katherine with unwashed hair and the smallest waist she'd ever seen, besides her own six months prior. Katherine watched as under-fleshed bones made pointed edges of a ratty, oversized tee shirt against the breeze. Katherine wanted to grab a spider-leg arm and say either that she used to be even pointier, or that it didn't have to be like it so obviously was, that whatever the girl - the woman - was afraid would happen if she softened, it wouldn't be nearly so bad as making a table was good, and maybe there was something even better in store for her than that. She stopped herself when she saw that the arm had a very important task: clutching a sugar-free iced tea. It was just like the kind Katherine used to buy. She knew what it was for. The eyes looked at her and Katherine looked back at the eyes and like recognized like and breaths hitched over that yellow-toothed scar-knuckled smile exchanged by people with equally bad judgement and something moved, she'd swear to God and all the angels that something moved in the girl's mouth, something soft and grey, and then they passed one another.

The windows to the corner store were all boarded up with thick splintery wood, but the sign on the door said

OPEN. SHOES REQUIRED.

It made sense to Katherine that there'd been break-ins. Of course, it was nobody's fault that her strongest memory of the time before the table was of pacing the aisles behind that sign and triple-checking the calorie counts on Chef Boyardee cans. It had happened, though, and it had happened there. She thought that maybe places where bad things happened attracted more bad things, like spiderwebs glittering with mosquito guts.

Everything did include sandpaper. She had a hard time believing the placement was coincidental. She knew that there were only so many shelves. Still. There was an obvious pattern to the bottle-shaped shadows cast by fridge light on the haphazard pile of red-stickered home repair items, and if only its meaning would reveal itself to her she might let go of the breath she'd been holding since she passed the girl—the woman.

She stooped down to pluck the packet off the shelf. Her back was cold. She turned around and looked the drinks machine up and down, and down and up.

She was going to hold one. She was not going to buy it. She certainly was not going to drink it. She put food in her stomach and she kept it there until it left naturally, and she was almost done making a table. She just wanted to feel the weight of the alternative sloshing around her palms for a second. For old times' sake.

She felt it on her face again, that gentle pull, almost indecipherable from the sensation of fridge air and fluorescent light, but only almost. It was there, whatever it was, tugging at her from underneath the blanket of toilet paper, cheap toys, and shelf dust. It was there.

The bottle was exactly the same size and shape she remembered. She closed her eyes with the plastic under her thumb, thinking that she wouldn't pick it up after all, that she wanted to turn around, go to the counter, pay for her sandpaper, and leave. *Do not pick up the bottle* she told herself.

There was nothing underneath the bottle. All around there was something—condensation, other bottles, air. Then: a perfect circle of total blankness, a grey fuzzy nothing. Freed from its bottle-capping, it did not pull gently, no, she was yanked face-first into it. Only the fat deposits on her hips kept her from blinking out of existence right there in the corner store.

The Nothing was a complete hunger. In the time before the table, she'd come to know hunger intimately, studied its rhythms beat for beat, wrote dissertations on the subject in the language of macronutrient ratios in the corners of all her papers, but never before this had it made itself a place for her to be in.

All around her were grey things, clear as day and no longer peripheral. They looked like slugs, but worse—stickier and shinier. They brushed her face with their hideous sheen, her neck, her eyelashes, and she wanted to die.

We bet the good stuff is on the other side. The hollow, collective voice of infinite Nothing creatures reverberated between her ears, giving her a terrible headache. *It's all skin and bone about the shoulders bring the hips in the thighs the tummy.*

"No." The second she opened her mouth, she wished she hadn't. The Nothing had an aftertaste like vomit.

Hips thighs tummy hips thighs tummy hips thighs tummy hips -

She closed her eyes and tried to picture the color red. It didn't come to her. In its place came the shock of cold air on her legs, and with it the memory that she *had* legs, that these legs were at that very moment in the corner store and out of the Nothing. She pushed her thighs against the machine until her left shoulder and arm came free, and used that to pull the rest of herself out. She fell unceremoniously on the floor, bruising her flabby ass and sending the iced tea bottle skittering. She crawled on hands and knees to retrieve it, stood up, opened the fridge door very carefully, and dropped the bottle on top of the Nothing. The pull relented. Mostly.

The fridge whirred on. A man argued with the cashier about the price of lottery tickets. A sequined scrunchie slithered into a preteen's pocket from between her fingers. There was just one thread out of place in the fabric of an afternoon at the neighborhood corner store, and that was something soft moving around her mouth, something that got in there when she was halfway to no place. She bought the sandpaper, pushing a few crumpled bills at the cashier without speaking, and thinking of the unfinished items on her checklist with a new urgency.

Cherry was in the hall again.

"Hello! Did you know that the human brain is almost 60% fat?"

Katherine didn't stop, even when the words *We did not know that interesting very interesting* thickly caked her mind.

The drill drove home the screws, attaching the top to the legs. The wood smoothed under her furiously moving palm. She worked in a concentric circle until the surface was totally even. Dragging her knuckles across the perfect smoothness, it occurred to her that she'd forgotten dinner. There were snacks in her fridge and in her pantry and she was allowed to eat them.

All that appealed to her was a bottle of mayo. She set it down on the counter and stood there cracking her neck, trying to decide what to squirt it on. The creature in her mouth sped up, bouncing on her tongue like a kid on a trampoline. The stale bread in the pantry would have to do.

A glob of fat seeped past the mouth of the tube, and the creature rammed hard into her front teeth, pushing her mouth open by the overbite. Soon there was no more mayo, in the bottle or otherwise. The creature slurped it all. It flew over to the pantry next, and the next thing she knew all of her cashews had disappeared into its rippling grey flesh. When it was done with those, it darted around, stopping to sniff the baggies of chips and containers of dry rice.

Instead of either, it devoured the wooden shelf, sending the rest of the food thereon toppling to the ground. She caught a glimpse of shining silver teeth, sharp and moving horizontally, and then it burped a cloud of sawdust and flew back into her mouth.

We don't do carbs give hips thighs tummy hips thighs tummy hips -

To drown this out, she got back to the table. The flesh of her hand caught on the jagged edge of the dye can when she pried it open. Blood mixed with artificial coloring and her apartment got heavy with the smell of the dye. Her stomach roiled. She rushed to the toilet and put both knees on the floor. The bleeding hand bunched her hair away from her face and the other braced on the seat. Déjà vu and nausea swirled around one another. When her lower lip wobbled, though, she felt the creature moving again, so she kept her mouth shut and she swallowed her stomach acid.

A knock at the door. She groaned from the ground, but the knock only got louder, and louder, and louder still, and she had to put a stop to it.

It was Cherry, holding her tray. The scents of cocoa and sugar cut through the dye vapors.

"Thank you for the cookies. I wanted to return the favor." Katherine nodded. Behind her tight-lipped grimace, the creature writhed. Cherry held out the brownies. The creature leapt up with enough force to swing Katherine's whole face up toward the ceiling, but she kept her teeth firmly gritted. She pushed against the pressure as hard as she could, which was just hard enough to look directly at the top of Cherry's head. She remembered the most recent *Did you know,* about the fat content of the human brain.

She grabbed the tray from Cherry's hands and lifted her arms. There was something sacramental about the pose, the metal sparkling dully in the fluorescent hallway light, the slight bend of her elbows. She did not get to contemplate the aesthetics further, though, because in a heartbeat it was over and the pan was upside down on Cherry's head. Its contents slopped onto her shoulders. A fleck of chocolate landed on her teal sock.

Just to be safe, Katherine reached out, scooped up a handful of the carb-protectorate, and smeared it across Cherry's forehead. The nothing creature went still. Through her nose, she heaved a sigh of relief.

"... Not a good time?" Cherry asked, blinking through the crumbs cascading into her eyes. Katherine walked backwards through her door and slammed it shut.

She managed to splash a layer of dye on the top of the table before the creature decided it would have more wood in the absence of hips, thighs, tummy, or brain. She was too tired to keep it in. It pushed her teeth apart, flew out, ate the whole table, and slung itself back into her mouth.

She didn't expect Cherry to come back any time soon. Even so, it seemed prudent to double check that she'd locked the door. When she went over, she saw that the checklist had flipped. She found herself looking at the old checklist, the one she'd tried to send to hell where it belonged six months before.

The inventory of pounds to lose needed some updating. The scale was deep in her storage closet, but not so deep that she couldn't find it, not so deep that she couldn't strip down and learn just how much updating, exactly, was needed.

She didn't like the number. The creature was getting antsy again, moving around. Sooner or later, she knew it was going to take something more substantial than mayonnaise or cashews or shelf or table. Unless she took it home first. She didn't like the number. They wouldn't fit in the Nothing with all the flesh on her sides, the two of them. She didn't like the number. The creature flung itself at the roof of her mouth again and she didn't fight it. She let it fly out and eat the skin and fat from her hips, and she watched the number get more likeable. It did her thighs next, then her abdomen. After this, it hovered in the air, grinding its silver teeth. She could tell from its posture it was thinking about her head.

"Can I keep it for just a little while longer?" She asked. She was neither begging nor demanding with the question. She was negotiating.

Hips thighs tummy wood wood wood do satisfy us for now we have already taken one of the pink thing we can wait for additional.

Back into her mouth it went.

The girl was outside once more, although the moon was high and the corner store was closed. In her haste she'd forgone shoes.

Gravel and bits of broken glass studded her bare feet. Katherine's sides and legs were red and wet. The girl didn't mind. She herself was red and wet at the shoulders. Katherine did not look at the back of her head. She knew what she would see if she did. They opened their mouths wide and from within twin creatures emerged and ate the window boards. The girl entered first, then turned, and extended a veiny hand. Katherine traced the bruises above the fingers and placed hers in it. The only light inside was that of the refrigerated drinks dispenser. Bottle-shaped shadows grew on their faces as they stumbled, bleeding and bony, to the sugar-free iced teas.

THANK YOU TO OUR SUPPORTERS

Many thanks to our patrons and supporters, especially:

Johanna Levene • Kathryn Parsons
Cathrin Hagey • Natalie Weizenbaum

Frederick Stark • Steven • Juliette McHardy • Kate Boyes
Alina Kanaski • Jeffery Reynolds • Myz Lilith
D.M. Domosea • carol shoemake • Erik DeBill
Bonnie Warford • Felicia OSullivan • Salomao Becker
Anna O'Brien • Martin Cohen • J'nae Spano • Tory Hoke
Matthew Bennardo • Kayla D

smokestack • Lisa Short • Leslie Anderson • Sian Jones
Kristina Saccone • Rocky B • BethOfAus • J. Askew
Dirck de Lint • Brit Hvide • Wanda • Karen Anderson
Charlotte Nash-Stewart • Jocelyn Actual • Carly Racklin
Liz Warner • Suzanne Thackston • Jen G
Emily Anderson • Maria Haskins • GriffinFire

Want to see your name here? Become a patron!
patreon.com/lunastation

About the Cover Artist

Amagoia Agirre is a freelance illustrator and comic artist based in Spain. Nature lover and fantasy narrative fan. Currently working on various illustrated books and comics as well as some personal projects.

lacont.artstation.com